THE OCEAN CHILD
OR THE LOST IVES

THE OCEAN CHILD.

A Domestic Tale.

BY THE AUTHOR OF "CLARISSE," "TEMPTATION," "PAUL THE RECKLESS," &c

CHAPTER I.

THE LOST SHIP.

NEVER had the indications of a coming storm been more apparent than this evening to which the commencement of our present narrative belongs. Mr. D——, the exemplary clergyman of a small parish on the sea-coast, had anxiously sought the beach to ascertain if any vessels were in sight, and as he stood in an open spot that commanded a wide expanse of ocean, he could see but too clearly tempest of more than ordinary violence was coming on. The red, unnatural glare of the setting sun formed an awful contrast with the huge black masses of clouds that rose from below the horizon, then, as they increased in number, formed themselves into one compact body, from which streams of light shone forth as if the elements were impatient to commence their work of destruction. The wind, too, which till now had been hushed, began to rise in all its terrible might, and the waves, yielding to its resistless powers, heaved and rolled onwards, as if to carry destruction to all within their sway.

Whilst Mr. Dawson stood watching the progress of the storm, the darkness of night came on, and it was only by the vivid flashes of the electric fluid that he could obtain occasional glimpses over the ocean. He, however, congratulated himself upon the apparent certainty that no vessels were lying off that dangerous coast, and as a heavy rain was coming on, he turned away to seek the shelter of his home, when a voice was heard calling him by name, and his servant came running with breathless haste towards him.

"Ah! sir," he exclaimed, "for pity's sake, come with me, and see if something can't be done to save the poor wretches that are in danger of foundering upon yonder rocks."

"Is there a vessel so near our coast?" asked Mr. Dawson, with alarm. "I have been watching from yonder rising ground, and as there was nothing in sight, I hoped we should have been spared the misery of witnessing a scene that but too frequently occurs on this treacherous coast."

"The ship lies round yonder headland," exclaimed Richard; "and I'm afraid, unless we can put some of our boats off, the crew and passengers will be lost."

Without waiting to ask any more questions, Mr. Dawson, in defiance of the heavy rain that had now come on, hurried off in the direction alluded to, and, followed by his faithful servant, soon reached the spot, where he found a number of the villagers and fishermen assembled, but not one of whom had at present made any effort to succour the unfortunate wretches, whose frantic screams filled the air, and added to the horrors of that dreadful night. By the vivid flashes of lightning, he could perceive the vessel, which was deprived of all its masts, and upon whose decks were crowded the despairing crew and passengers. The good pastor shuddered as this fearful sight was presented to his view, and addressing himself to the spectators on the beach, he inquired if no efforts could be made to rescue the unfortunates from their perilous situation.

"We have been thinking of putting off a boat or two, your honour," replied one of the men, who acted as spokesmen for the rest; "but the sea runs so high, with the wind dead ashore, that we should only be risking our lives without a chance of doing any good to the people aboard yonder doomed ship."

"Are there none among you," asked the clergyman, in despair, "that will make an effort, in such a fearful emergency as this?"

"Why, for that matter," cried the fisherman, "we are all ready enough to lend a helping hand; but we have wives and families depending on us for support, and if we should be drowned, the poor helpless creatures must starve or go to the workhouse, and either of 'em is bad enough, as you must own."

"But you have been out in many a night as rough as this?" observed Mr. Dawson.

"That's very true, sir," answered the man; "but there's a difference between being caught in a storm and putting out to sea when everything's against us."

"Will none of you make an effort to save them?" said Mr. Dawson, as another fearful scream issued from the devoted ship. "Are ye men that ye can hear the cry of distress, yet hesitate to save the lives of your suffering fellow-creatures?"

No reply was made to the appeal, and, as a last resource, he added,—

"If money be your object, I will myself reward every man that ventures to put off in his boat. Say, are there any among you that will earn gold by an attempt to take off the unfortunate people from yonder vessel?"

No answer was made to the reproachful question; but some of the people moved sullenly to the water's edge, and began to get ready a couple of boats that seemed best adapted to weather the storm. But all was unavailing, for a heavy surf was running in, and scarcely had the adventurers put off than the frail vessels were overturned, and the crews, with extreme difficulty, succeeded in buffetting their way to the shore.

Mr. Dawson now despaired of rendering any assistance to those on board the fatal vessel; but, shortly afterwards, he could see, by the almost incessant flashes of lightning, that some boats, filled with people, had just left the ship, and were making towards the shore. With intense anxiety, the spectators watched the frail barks as they were dashed about at the mercy of wind and waves. Few believed it possible that they could weather such a tempest, and too soon, alas! the fatal prognostication was confirmed, for in the brief interval of darkness that occurred between the flashes of lightning, a harrowing scream was heard, and when the ocean was again illumined, the boats had disappeared, and not a soul was seen struggling in the waters that were doomed to be their grave! A groan of insupportable anguish burst from the lips of Mr. Dawson, and burying his face in his hands, he was wrapped in the harrowing thoughts that agitated his heart.

Though all hope of rescuing any of the crew or passengers was at an end, Mr. Dawson could not be prevailed on to leave the spot; for shortly after the upsetting of the boats, the storm began to relax some of its violence, and he resolved to stay and see whether there might not be some to whom assistance could be afforded. However, many of the spectators of this melancholy scene left the place to return home, though a good many still remained with the clergyman to give him their assistance in case it should be required. By this time the rain had very much subsided, and those who yet waited on the beach strolled up and down to see if any of the bodies had been washed ashore, and to afford timely aid ___ se any should be found in whom the spark of life was not quite extinct.

Nearly one hour had been spent in this fruitless search, when a sudden exclamation from Mr. Dawson drew all eyes towards him, and it was seen that h attention had been attracted towards something that was floating on the waters a no great distance off. All immediately gathered about Mr. Dawson to know if he had any orders to give as to what they should now do; but by this time the object of their wonder was close at hand, and before he could issue any directions upon the subject, a wave dashed at their feet the body of a woman, who, though evid tly dead, clasped in her arms an infant that seemed to be but a few weeks of age. A deep feeling of anxiety now filled every breast to ascertain if any assistance could avail to restore animation, but the hapless mother was beyond all human aid; though the child, upon being removed from her tight embrace, showed some slight signs of animation that afforded ground for hoping that one at least would be saved out of the numerous victims of the raging tempest.

"Child of the ocean!" exclaimed Mr. Dawson, "Heaven has committed thee to my care, and if thy life is spared thou shalt be to me as a beloved daughter."

"The child seems likely enough to recover, sir," observed the fisherman who had acted as spokesman on the previous occasion; "but as for the poor woman, here, I'm afraid it's all over with her."

"Let every care be taken of her," said Mr. Dawson. "In all probability she is the mother of this beauteous babe, and it would be some consolation to us could we preserve the lives of two persons out of all who have fallen victims to this terrible storm."

"I'm afraid it's no use, sir," exclaimed the other, who by this time had removed the body higher up the beach so as to be out of the way of the waves. "She seems to be quite dead, and I rather think the only trouble she'll give anybody will be to lay her in the grave."

"She must be removed to my house," said the clergyman, "where medical assistance must be immediately summoned. Yet I fear all will be in vain, for the pulse has entirely ceased to beat, and the coldness of death is upon her."

"Hadn't you better let some of our women take care of the child at present?" asked the fisherman.

"No," he replied; "it is a sacred trust imposed upon me, and never, from this time, shall the infant leave my protection. The mother, I fear, is past all human help, but for Heaven's sake, leave no effort untried till you have ascertained whether a spark of life remains."

" She's not dead !" exclaimed Richard, who had been kneeling over the body to see if all was indeed over.

" Are you sure of it ?" demanded his master, eagerly advancing.

" Quite sure, sir," was the quick response. " She sighed deeply, and partly opened her eyes, though she closed them again almost directly afterwards. If anybody, now, had such a thing as a drop of brandy, and we could get a little of it down her throat, I shouldn't wonder if it brought her back to life."

" If that's the case, you'll find a little in this bottle," said the fisherman, offering an almost empty flask. " There ain't much in it, to be sure, but what there is the poor woman's quite welcome to, if it only does her good."

A very small quantity was poured down the unfortunate woman's throat, and after a convulsive struggle she uttered a deep sigh and opened her languid eyes, as if to look round for the child. Mr. Dawson guessed as much, and placed the infant before her, but the power of vision seemed to have failed her, and again closing her eyes, she once more resumed all the appearance of death ; yet in that brief interval she uttered three or four words in a foreign language, but this was done in so low a tone, that, with all his anxiety, Mr. Dawson was unable to satisfy himself with respect to the country to which she belonged. Still, however, he hoped she might recover sufficiently to throw some light upon the child's family and connexions ; but the wish was a vain one, for shortly afterwards she was seized with convulsions and expired in the arms of those who had raised her head, when it was believed she was going to speak.

As nothing more could be done, Mr. Dawson gave directions for the corse to be taken, with as little delay as possible, to his house, in order that it might be interred, with all the decency and respect that it was in his power to bestow. Having made this arrangement, he left them, and pressing the infant to his bosom, he exclaimed ardently,—

" My poor child, thou hast lost her who was thy natural protector, yet shalt thou find a friend who will never abandon thee while he has a crust to share with the lone orphan. The raging tempest has spared thee when all else perished, and from this time forward I will rear thee in tenderness and love as if thou hadst been my own daughter."

On arriving at home he was met by his kind-hearted sister, to whom he briefly related the events of the night, and then consigned the infant to her care, with a strict injunction that everything should be done which its helplessness required. Miss Isabel Dawson was highly delighted with her young charge, and readily promised that the greatest care should be taken of it ; and her brother, being thus far satisfied that he had faithfully performed a solemn duty, retired to his study, where in solitude and quiet he might reflect on the singular event, and form projects as to the course that should be adopted towards discovering who were the parents of his young charge.

In the morning, his sister reported to him that, having seen the woman's body, she was of opinion that she was too old to be the mother of the infant who had been so providentially rescued from destruction. Of her religion there could be no doubt, since a missal, rosary, and cross were found in her pockets, and from the few foreign coins she had about her, there was good reason to believe that she was not a native of England. But upon this point no certain conclusion could be formed, for during the night the ship had gone to the bottom, carrying with it every vestige that might have afforded the slightest clue towards unravelling the mystery.

" Heaven only knows," Mr. Dawson said to his sister, " whether the relatives of this poor child will ever be discovered ; but, at any rate, we must use every precaution to keep together what little evidence we may happen to possess. The few things found in the pockets of the woman, together with her clothes, and those belonging to the child, must be put away and preserved, in case they should hereafter be necessary to corroborate any further testimony that time may bring forward."

"That's exactly what I have been thinking myself," replied the maiden lady, who generally made it a rule to fall into her brother's notions. "We must, of course, take care of everything belonging to them, and as a proof that I was not unmindful upon the subject, I have sent into the village for new clothing, to supply the place of that which the infant now wears."

"You are a kind, thoughtful creature," exclaimed Mr. Dawson; "and if one thing more than another could increase my fraternal regard for you, it is the readiness with which you have undertaken a task that, for the first few years of childhood, must prove rather a troublesome one."

"Ay," answered Miss Isabel; "but think of the comfort she may be to us as she grows up. She will be to me as a daughter, and will not that be a reward for all the watchful anxiety that helpless infancy requires?"

"True," replied the clergyman; "but how few are there, my dear sister, who would voluntarily take upon themselves a duty such as you have imposed upon yourself. The world, I am sorry to say, is selfish, and had this poor babe been cast upon the charity of ninety-nine persons out of a hundred, it might have been sent to the workhouse to wear out the remainder of its days in poverty and neglect."

Miss Isabel made no reply to the praise thus bestowed upon her by the clergyman, but having asked his advice on various subjects, respecting the child, she left the room to commence the duties she had benevolently taken upon herself. Mr. Dawson smiled at the zeal thus manifested by his maiden sister, but he could firmly rely on her faithfully discharging them, and never did he feel happier, than in the consciousness of having fulfilled the duty of a Christian teacher.

CHAPTER II.

A WEIGHTY CONSIDERATION.

THE truly excellent clergyman who had thus undertaken to fulfil the duties of a parent to the child whom chance had thrown in his way, was a widower of about the middle age of life. About a year and a-half before the commencement of our narrative, he had the affliction to lose a beloved wife, whose many estimable qualities had endeared her to him beyond all other treasures that he possessed. This bereavement deeply affected him, and it was evident that he became a prey to grief that required all his fortitude to conceal from those who felt an interest in his behalf. There were few, indeed, to whom he would ever venture to broach the subject; but his sister and the faithful attendant that we have already introduced to our readers, could see that he grew more retired in his habits than had been his wont, and the sorrowful expression of his countenance spoke, as plainly as words could have done, of the silent woe with which he still lamented the loss of a beloved companion.

His family consisted of one child, a boy about five years of age, his sister, who was now entrusted with the management of his household, a couple of female domestics, and worthy Richard Martin, a sort of useful man in the establishment, occupying himself sometimes as gardener, sometimes as messenger, and, in fact, just doing any little things that were required, in order to keep a situation that it would have broken his heart to leave.

The living held by Mr. Dawson was far from being a very profitable one, but as his wants were few, and his sister was a clever manager, he contrived to support himself in a degree of respectability that obtained for him the friendship and admiration of all who had the happiness of enjoying his acquaintance. Contented with his lot, he felt no anxiety for any further preferment, and it is, indeed, doubtful whether he would have occupied a richer living, since it would compel him to leave the flock to whom he had grown attached, from long residence among them.

Miss Isabel Dawson was a placid maiden lady of nearly his own age, but without any pretensions to more than an ordinary share of understanding. The goodness of her heart, however, was daily manifested in the zeal with which she sought to make herself acquainted with all cases of distress, and the promptitude with which she afforded assistance to those who required it.   By the villagers she was regarded as a Lady Bountiful, and the respect they paid her was commensurate with the many generous acts that were recorded of her.   Retired in her habits, she had no wish to mix with the gay society that would have joyfully received her, and the consequence was that her visits were almost entirely restricted to the humble dwellings of those whose troubles and misfortunes it was her chief pleasure to alleviate.

Little Frank Dawson, the vicar's only child, was a high-spirited boy, though, at the period we allude to, he had numbered only five years.   Though coming under the denomination of an old maid, aunt Isabel was excessively fond of the child, and, as his father thought, indulged him a great deal more than she ought to do. Her over partiality was not without its evil effects upon the boy; but the steady watchfulness of the father served as a curb to the somewhat boisterous spirit of the child, and Mr. Dawson consoled himself with the reflection, that as Frank grew older, he would become more tractable to the solemn counsels of a parent.   To his aunt the child was evidently attached, obeying her in all things with the utmost readiness, and shedding tears of unfeigned sorrow, if at any time he so far offended as to incur her severe displeasure.

Fearful, however, lest the boy should be irretrievably spoiled by this over indulgence, Mr. Dawson came to the determination of sending him to a school a few miles from the vicarage, in the hope of preventing an evil, the contemplation of which afforded him so much uneasiness.   This resolution was no sooner formed than acted on, and in spite of all the remonstrances of aunt Isabel, the boy was sent away, with an understanding that, except in case of illness, he should never visit home but at the regular vacations.   This occurred only a few weeks before the fatal shipwreck, and no sooner did the orphan child make her appearance in the family of Mr. Dawson, than she bade fair to take little Frank's place in the affections of good aunt Isabel, who, for a whole week afterwards, puzzled her brains to think of some pretty name for the infant to whom she intended to be god-mother. This, however, was a knotty point that she was unable to decide upon, and it was therefore at length determined that she should consult her brother, to whose opinion, in all such weighty matters, she usually bowed with deference.

But it so happened that, at this time, Mr. Dawson confined himself more than ever to the solitude of his study, and Miss Isabel only met him at their meals, when he seemed disposed to talk upon any other subjects rather than the one she was so very anxious to confer about.   In fact, he knew that among her few foibles she was rather apt to prove a bore on certain subjects, and dreading the bare idea of getting into an argument with her, he constantly changed the theme, as often as she commenced a disquisition upon the choice of names.

At last, however, she determined to bring the matter to an issue, and having quietly submitted for a long time to his usual tactics, she resolved upon coming boldly to the point.

"I have been trying, my dear brother," she said, "to get your opinion upon what I conceive to be a very important affair.   In short, this poor child must have a name, and ——"

"What name?" interrupted Mr. Dawson.

"Ah! that's the very thing I wanted to speak to you about," she replied.   "I have thought of at least five hundred, and yet, after all, have not been able to make up my mind about it."

"The choice of a name is surely hardly worth so much trouble," observed the clergyman, smiling at the importance she attached to it.

"But we may as well choose a pretty one, while we are about it."

"Exactly so," answered Mr. Dawson; "and, having been given to us by the sea, what say you to the name of Oceana?"

"Too fine, a great deal," replied the lady; "besides, I am afraid very few people would understand what it means.   Oceana sounds pretty, to be sure, but I'm afraid we should be terribly laughed at if we gave her such a fine name as that."

See page 14.

"Well," laughed her brother, "I was only trying to get at your opinion on the subject ; and, to confess the truth, I have been somewhat troubled myself to hit upon a name for our little foundling."

"And have you succeeded in pleasing yourself?"

"On the contrary, I am as far off as ever."

"It's strange, too, that we should find so much difficulty about a mere trifle," observed Miss Isabel, after a pause. "For my own part, I have not been able to fix my choice, and so, if you please, we'll have the child brought in, and perhaps something may strike us when we are looking at her."

"Or, perhaps," said Mr. Dawson, "the baby may make a choice for herself."

"At any rate, she may as well be present at our conference," observed the lady, and ringing the bell for a servant, she desired the little stranger to be brought in. The order was instantly obeyed, and, as she took the infant from her nurse, she said,—

"I wish to goodness, my dear brother, we could guess the country of its birth."

"A very useless wish," observed Mr. Dawson, "seeing that we may guess for a whole lifetime without coming a bit nearer the mark."

"Don't you think it's very likely she was born in Italy?" asked his sister.

"As likely as not," he replied; "but I cannot conceive why you should hit upon that country any more than another."

"I fancied so," returned Miss Isabel, "because there's no doubt about her friends being Roman Catholics, and I believe there's nothing else but people of that religion over there. If I was only certain of it, I should propose that we call her Virginia."

"But not being certain of it," exclaimed Mr. Dawson, "I think we had better fix upon some name that's not quite so romantic. She may be from France, Spain, Portugal, or any other country for aught we know. Nay, for that matter, how can we tell but she may be an English child?"

"That's very unlikely," retorted Miss Isabel, "for you told me that just before the poor woman expired, she pronounced some words in a foreign language."

"She did," answered Mr. Dawson, "but what the words were I have not been able to make out. She spoke in a faint, exhausted tone, and while I was anxiously waiting to hear her again, she sank back and left us in all the darkness of uncertainty."

"What a pity it is she could not make herself understood," said the lady, who was not without a very good share of female curiosity. "Had a little more time been spared her, what an immense deal of trouble and anxiety it would have saved us."

"The best way is to let the thing take its chance," exclaimed Mr. Dawson. "For my own part, I see no use in puzzling our brains with a parcel of useless surmises, so the wisest plan will be to wait till something like a probability turns up in our favour, and then, with the slightest clue in the world, we may pursue our inquiries with some chance of arriving at a satisfactory conclusion."

"Do you think such a chance is ever likely to happen?" asked his sister.

"Strange events have occurred before now," he replied; "and why not in favour of our young charge as well as anybody else?"

"That's very true," acquiesced Miss Isabel, "so we'll wait patiently, and perhaps by-and-by we shall see something in the newspapers about the ship that was lost. If we can only find out the country it came from, it would be easy to learn the names of the passengers, and then what is to hinder us from tracing out the parentage of this poor babe? But we are forgetting what we first of all began to talk about, and if we go on at this rate, the child is likely enough to have no name after all my anxiety."

"Can't you suggest anything for my approval?" asked her brother.

"Why, there's one name that I thought would be rather applicable," replied Miss Isabel; "but as it's a fine one, I don't know but you will laugh at me if I tell you."

"What is it?"

"You shall hear," she replied; "but in the first place I must remind you that she was rescued from death on a night in the month of July."

"Exactly so."

"Well then, I would propose the name of Julia, and I think if we were to ponder over the affair for a month to come, we could not fix upon a prettier or more appropriate name. Why, I declare, brother, if the child don't smile as if in approval of what I have been saying, and so, with your leave, we'll come to an understanding that the point is settled."

"Ay, ay, Julia, let it be," said Mr. Dawson, heartily glad to bring the consultation to an end.

"And I will be one of its god-mothers mind."

"Certainly," replied Mr. Dawson; "no one that I am acquainted with is better adapted for such a duty, and the only condition I shall extort, is, that you will not spoil the girl as you did my little Frank."

"Humouring children a little don't always spoil them," answered Miss Isabel, sharply, " and as for poor Frank, if I did allow him to have his own way now and then, he's suffering for it by being sent away from his own natural protectors."

" I trust the child is where he will be well taken care of."

" Oh, yes, they'll feed him well, and stuff his head with all sorts of learning," replied the lady, " but what consolation is there in all that, if he gets whipped and punished for every trifling fault he may be guilty of ? Besides, the boys are all bigger than he is, so that if they offend him he will be obliged to put up with it, instead of showing a little spirit as he used to do."

" It has been my opinion for some time past," replied Mr. Dawson, " that the boy showed a great deal too much spirit, and that was my chief motive for sending him where he might mix with children rather older than himself. He will thus be obliged to lower his tone or run the chance of meeting with a little wholesome chastisement. Believe me, the plan I have adopted is a very excellent one to correct the evil habits he has formed at home."

" Evil habits, brother !" exclaimed Miss Isabel, sharply.

" Nay, pardon me, if I have said anything to offend," exclaimed Mr. Dawson, who found that she took his last few words to herself. " You were always partial to the boy—too partial, I may say—and therein is the secret of his being spoilt. However, he is now removed beyond the reach of your mistaken kindness, and now that another little favourite has come in the way, I suppose she will stand a chance of being spoilt as he was."

" Brother !" cried Miss Isabel; " if I was not blessed with a tolerable good temper, you would provoke me to say something in reply."

'It would not be anything very severe I am sure," he replied, " for you and I have lived together too long to quarrel about trifles. Besides, is not death beneath our roof, and would it not be unseemly were we to wrangle almost in the presence of the dead ?"

" I am never angry but when I think of poor Frank, and the hardships he must endure through being sent from home," replied Miss Isabel. " As for the little foundling putting his nose out of joint, that's quite a matter of impossibility, for, though I shall love her as my own child, it will not be at the expense of my own nephew. But things will go on differently after to-morrow, for the funeral will then be over, and then things can go on in their own way again."

" And the christening of the child follows," said Mr. Dawson, with a sigh. " Such are the scenes and changes that meet us at every turn in life ! some leave the world, and others find their way into it to pass through a weary pilgrimage that terminates in the grave ! But this is a serious reflection, Isabel, and I will pursue it no further since I see it makes you melancholy. We have settled the knotty point between us, and unless your mind changes again, the young stranger will receive the name of Julia."

" Ay, that is the name."

" But what surname shall she be known by ?" asked Mr. Dawson.

" Why, our own to be sure," answered the lady ; " we don't know of any other to give her, and till something can be discovered respecting her family, the name of Dawson will do as well as any other."

" Julia Dawson," murmured the clergyman to himself. " Well, well, I see no reasonable objection to your suggestion, so she shall receive my name till the time comes when we know her real one."

" Do you think that will ever happen ?" asked his sister, eagerly.

" We may at least hope so," answered Mr. Dawson ; " and as far as lies in my power, I shall endeavour to set the question at rest. The task, I expect, will be a difficult one, but I shall not flinch from it while I can see the faintest probability of success."

" And if I can be of any service," added Miss Isabel, " you may command me whenever or however you think proper. I have patience and perseverance enough when there's occasion to call them into practice, and even if it were necessary to travel half over the world, I would undertake the labour for the sake of this poor orphan child."

"That is spoken like yourself, my dear sister," exclaimed Mr. Dawson, warmly; "your words sound grateful to my ears; and, rely upon it, I will not fail to seek your counsel and assistance, should I ever succeed in obtaining the clue I so anxiously look forward to."

He pressed her hand as he said this, and again committing the child to her especial care and protection, left the room. Miss Isabel then gave the young foundling to the care of its nurse, and as the next day was appointed for the funeral of the unfortunate stranger, she busily occupied herself in making the necessary preparations.

CHAPTER III.

A CLAIMANT.

THE next day, which happened to be Sunday, was a peculiarly solemn one at the vicarage, for the remains of the unfortunate woman who had lost her life in the tempest were to be consigned to their last earthly resting-place. Miss Isabel took her place at the breakfast table that morning with a countenance expressive of the most poignant grief, and it was not till her brother had spoken several times that she could make him any reply.

"I scarcely know how it is," she said, "but I am as much a prey to grief as if the poor creature we are about to lay in the grave had been a sister, or highly esteemed friend."

"It is easily accounted for," observed Mr. Dawson. "The child has already become a favourite, and you naturally feel regret for the fate of one who was either its mother or very nearly connected."

"Yet she might not have been either," replied the lady, after a pause.

"Nay, I am sure she was."

"Upon what ground do you form your opinion?"

"On that of the evident affection with which she regarded the child," replied Mr. Dawson. "When they were cast upon the beach, the arms of the woman were firmly clasped round the infant, and though life was nearly extinct, she held her young charge with a tenacity of grasp that clearly proved her intense anxiety to preserve it, even though she might herself perish. And on reviving a little, she seemed to observe with joy that the babe was not without protectors, and I am in hopes it might have soothed the last few moments of her existence."

"Well, I hope it did, poor soul," observed Miss Isabel; "for she must have needed consolation in such an awful hour as that. To be thrown among strangers, in a foreign land, is bad enough, but to die without one person near that you know, must be horrible indeed."

"And the more so," exclaimed her brother, "when the poor creature was uncertain what would be the fate of the child. It is to be hoped, however, that she was tolerably well assured on that point, for she saw me with the infant in my arms, and perhaps felt assured that the helpless babe was not left in the wide world without one that was ready to be its protector. Alas! to-day the grave closes upon her, and when the last mournful rites have been solemnised, I shall have the more agreeable task of admitting the babe into our flock."

"I am glad," said Miss Isabel, "that you have arranged for the funeral to take place in the morning, and the christening in the afternoon, because the first ceremony could not but have thrown a gloom over the other. As it is, the day will appear sad enough, but the gloom will soon wear off, and then we shall have nothing else to think about but our young charge, who, I doubt not, will hereafter reward our care with gratitude and love."

Breakfast being over, Mr. Dawson set off for the church, having first given orders for the funeral to start from his house immediately upon its being ascertained that the sermon was concluded. That morning Miss Isabel remained at home to see that everything was done according to her brother's instructions. Though a stranger to the deceased, she felt as much real sorrow as if they had been friends all their lives, and when Mr. Dawson returned home after the mournful ceremony had been completed, he found his sister absorbed in grief, and weeping bitterly for the fate of the hapless woman whom the fury of the tempest had sent to a premature grave. The reasoning of the good pastor, however, served to check the violence of her grief, and in the afternoon she accompanied the christening party to church, took upon herself the office of one of the sponsors, and almost forgot the sorrows of the morning in the joyful occasion that had so quickly succeeded it.

That evening Mr. Dawson retired to his chamber at an earlier hour than usual, and on the following day, glad to escape from the melancholy thought that oppressed him, he ordered his horse to be saddled, and set out with the intention of making a call at the school where little Frank was to receive the rudiments of education. Of course aunt Isabel had a thousand messages and presents to her young favourite, and her brother was not suffered to take his departure till his pockets were as full of cakes and toys, as his head was of kind messages, that he was strictly charged on no account to forget.

Scarcely had he gone, than a loud knocking at the hall door announced the arrival of a visitor, and presently afterwards Susan came running with breathless haste to announce the arrival of Squire Oakley from Morland-park.

" Did you tell him your master was not at home ?" asked Miss Isabel.

" I did, ma'am," replied the girl; " but he only gave a view halloo, such as they do when they're hunting the fox, and said, with an oath, that if the master was out, he supposed he must be satisfied with seeing the mistress."

" I would rather have seen anybody else," cried the lady, with evident signs of vexation. " He is so rough and boisterous in his way, that I always avoid him as I would a pestilence."

" Shall I send him to you, ma'am ?" asked Susan.

" No, tell him I am particularly engaged."

" I did, ma'am; but he said that was always the way with ladies when they don't want to see visitors; and when I said you were really very much occupied with particular business, he bade me tell you that he was not in any great hurry, and would wait till you were at leisure."

" How very provoking to be sure," cried Miss Isabel. " Do you think, Susan, you can make any excuse to get rid of him ?"

" He won't hear anything like an excuse," replied Susan. " I said as much to him as I dared, and he told me that he came on business, and wouldn't go away till he had settled it."

" Then I suppose I must go and see him," exclaimed her mistress, and having recovered her composure, she proceeded to the parlour, where she found Squire Oakley striding up and down with all the impatience of a chafed lion. Upon seeing her, however, his countenance brightened up, and uttering a tremendous shout, he grasped her boisterously by both hands.

" Yoicks! yoicks! here she is—here she is!" he vociferated, as if he was engaged in the chase. " How are you, miss—how are you? Gad! so the parson's stole away, eh? sly fox, ma'am—sly fox; but never mind, I suppose it will be all the same if I tell my business to you ?"

" I think you had better call again when my brother is at home," said Miss Isabel, quietly.

" No, ma'am, you'll do just as well," exclaimed the squire; " I've come to have a peep at your findings. They tell me the waves have made you a present of something worth the looking at. Do you make an exhibition of it, ma'am, at so much a head, or may I be allowed to look at it out of the old friendship we bear one another ?"

" I really don't understand what you mean, sir !" cried the lady, with surprise depicted in her countenance.

" Oh, stuff!" he exclaimed, rudely. " Haven't I heard that your brother saved something from the shipwreck the other night, and as lord of the manor, haven't I right to all waifs and strays ?"

" I don't know much about waifs and strays, as you call them," answered

Miss Isabel; "but the only thing my brother saved from the ship is an infant that is too young to stray."

"An infant!" exclaimed the squire, with amazement.

"Yes, sir," replied the lady; "a little girl that I should think is scarcely two months old. My brother saved it from the fury of the waves, and has resolved to rear it as his own, unless any one can prove a greater right to the infant."

"Is it pretty?" asked Squire Oakley.

"Very."

"Don't you know who it belongs to?"

"I am afraid there is no chance of our ever making that discovery," answered Miss Isabel.

"Why shouldn't you be able to find out the father and mother?"

"Because," she replied, "there is too much reason to believe that everybody in the ship perished. The child, when first discovered, was found fast locked in the arms of a woman, but whether she was the mother we have unfortunately no means of ascertaining."

"Is she dead?"

"Yes; and was buried yesterday in our church."

"Upon my life it's a strange thing that I shouldn't have heard something about this before now," exclaimed Oakley.

"Perhaps your people thought that the mere circumstance of a wreck was beneath your notice," said Miss Isabel, ironically.

"Likely enough—likely enough," replied the squire, cracking his whip till it rang again in the ears of the sensitive Miss Dawson. "However, I'll make some of their backs smart, I'll warrant you, for not telling me of this sooner; so let me see this child, Miss Isabel, for I like young 'uns when they're pretty, as you say this is."

To have raised any objection to this would, she knew perfectly well, be useless, and ringing the bell, she desired little Julia to be brought into the room. The order was immediately obeyed; and the squire, in spite of all his roughness of manner, could not help expressing his admiration of the child, which had been so providentially rescued from a watery grave.

"Upon my life," he exclaimed, "it would have been a thousand pities if such a smiling, good-tempered looking babe as this had gone to the bottom with the rest."

"It is, indeed, a beautiful infant," answered Miss Isabel, highly flattered by the notice bestowed on her young favourite. "My brother has grown quite fond of it already, and I really think loves it as well as he does his own child."

"Psha! What does he want with two of 'em?" asked Oakley; "one's enough for a person to bring up, I'm sure; so tell him he must let me have the girl, and I'll bring it up as my own."

"It would break my brother's heart to part with it," cried Miss Isabel; "indeed, sir, I am sure nothing would induce him to trust the child to the care of any other person."

"Well, I must talk to him about it, at any rate."

"I'm sure it will not be of any use, sir," exclaimed Miss Isabel Dawson, alarmed at the bare possibility of losing her young pet. "My brother saved the child, and of course has most right to become its protector."

"Well, upon second thoughts, I don't know but you may be in the right," said Squire Oakley; "but if it had been a boy instead of a girl, I should not have been quite so easily persuaded against it. There's that harum-scarum nephew of mine running through his money like a fool, as he is, and as I don't choose to have a spendthrift for my heir, I would have adopted this child if it had been a boy instead of a girl."

"That," observed Miss Dawson, in her usual quiet way, "would, I presume, have depended upon whether my brother would have been inclined to give up his right."

"Pooh! pooh! What right can he claim greater than my own?" demanded the other. "I am lord of the manor, I tell you, and that would have given me power over the child, as having been cast ashore on my property."

"In that case," said Miss Isabel, pointedly, "you might as well have claimed the body of the poor woman who died, and then, among other privileges, you would have had that of burying her at your own expense."

"Hang me, if I don't, somehow, always get the worst of it if I enter into an argument with the ladies," exclaimed Oakley, laughing heartily at the new light in which she had placed the affair. "However, we'll say no more about waifs and strays on the present occasion, so just tell your brother that he may keep the child, for anything I care about it, and if he should happen to find the expense too great, I don't mind paying a share of it, for old friendship's sake. So now good morning to you, Miss Isabel, and I dare say, if the truth was known, you'll be glad enough to get rid of me, for, somehow, all the women folks seem to think me a bit of a bore."

Squire Oakley shook her hand, as if he meant to squeeze it to a jelly, and having reiterated all that he wished to be said to Mr. Dawson, he left the vicarage, and, whistling to half a dozen dogs that had accompanied him, he returned home, thinking of the young foundling, and pondering in his own mind how he could best offer a sum of money towards defraying expenses without giving offence to Mr. Dawson.

With all his singularity of character, Squire Oakley possessed many excellent qualities that made him a great favourite in the neighbourhood. He was rich—the whole parish, in fact, belonged to him—and his mansion at Morland Park was always thrown open to those who chose to claim his hospitality. In early life he had met with a disappointment in love, and to that circumstance, perhaps, may be attributed the eccentricities that rendered his character so remarkable. When quite a youth, he quarrelled with his elder brother, who had succeeded to the title and estates of the Earl of Mayfield; and, from the period of their first estrangement, neither of them made any advances towards a reconciliation. The longer they remained thus separated, the more inveterate did Oakley grow in his hatred, and his rage became yet greater when he found that his estates must descend to his nephew, a son of the Earl of Mayfield, in the event of his not leaving male issue to inherit them. This was a sore subject with the squire, and, to do him justice, he left no efforts untried to discover if means might not be found out to prevent his property going to one who he hated no less for his extravagance and profligacy, than for his being the son of a person whose name and existence he would willingly have forgotten.

All, however, was of no avail, and it was the opinion of all the lawyers he had consulted upon the subject that his nephew must succeed to his estates, unless he chose to marry, and thus leave an heir who would effectually destroy all the pretensions of the other.

But by this time he was not by any means young, and having, as we have before said, formed a distaste for matrimony in consequence of an early disappointment, he thought the remedy almost as bad as the disease. Resolved, however, to take a wife, he at last chose the daughter of one of his tenants, and as she happened to be a woman of coarse and vulgar manners, he had soon reason to repent the hour when he involved himself in a matrimonial engagement. Constant broils and quarrels were the consequence; and being driven, as it were, from the enjoyments of home, he entered, heart and soul, into sporting pursuits, and was thus chiefly engaged in out-door amusements, instead of remaining at home, where he was sure to endure the miseries he had brought upon himself by an ill-assorted match. But most misfortunes come to an end some time or other, and those of Squire Oakley were not an exception. His wife burst a blood vessel in one of her fits of passion, and though medical assistance was speedily obtained, she died within a week afterwards, the victim of her own violent passion.

"Once bitten, twice shy," is an old adage that Squire Oakley often repeated, and, as may be supposed, he never again ventured to take unto himself a better half. The marriage had proved a fruitless one—no heir had made his appearance to the discomfiture of his much-hated nephew, and Squire Oakley had still the mortification of knowing that his property must descend to one towards whom he felt the most inveterate dislike.

In this situation there was only one way by which he could revenge himself. Doubtless his nephew must succeed him, but it was still in his own power to injure the property almost to any extent he pleased. Long leases, at very low rents, were granted to all the tenants, and if they thought proper to till the land badly, so as to deteriorate it in value, no remonstrance was made while they paid their rent with any regularity. Thus the estate was going rapidly to decay, and Squire Oakley would frequently chuckle to himself at the reflection that his nephew would not get much the best of him after all.

The vicarage, of which Mr. Dawson was the incumbent, also belonged to Oakley; and it was with a similar feeling which had actuated his former conduct, that he considered how he might prevent his heir from gaining any emolument from it, in the event of the present vicar's death. With this view, he offered to be at the expense of Frank Dawson's education, on condition that he was brought up for the church, and on arriving at the proper age his father was to resign the living in his son's favour, and either to have another one given him, or to receive an annuity equivalent to the proceeds of the vicarage. Mr. Dawson would rather have declined having anything to do with a quarrel that he would willingly have assisted to heal; but Oakley was determined, and at length the arrangement was made, and the squire could then exult in the complete accomplishment of the design he had been at so much pains to bring about.

The explanation we have thus given is rather long, but it was necessary for the development of our narrative, as will be seen as we proceed further in this most veracious history.

CHAPTER IV.

FRIENDLY COUNSEL.

MR. CAPEL, to whom the care of Frank Dawson was entrusted, was one of those unfortunate country curates who are expected to take all the labour from their well-paid vicars and rectors, in consideration of receiving a salary averaging about half as much as may be earned by a carpenter or bricklayer. Yet, though hard worked and ill paid, Mr. Capel was contented with his lot; but his income being found insufficient to support him in a respectable station, he took a limited number of young gentlemen to prepare them for college. With this assistance he was enabled to raise himself above the want that he must otherwise have endured; and by care and strict attention he contrived to limit his expenses within his means,—kept free from debt, and consequently was respected by all who knew him. Fortunately, too, he was blessed with a prudent, careful wife, to whose good management he owed no small share of the success he had met with.

To these people it was that Mr. Dawson paid a visit; for he generally consulted them whenever he found any difficulty in the way, and he was now anxious to hear what advice they would give with respect to the means that ought to be taken for discovering the relations of little Julia; if, indeed, any of them were fortunate enough not to have been on board the ill-fated vessel which had lately gone down.

" I have thought over a variety of schemes," he said; "some of which seem reasonable enough at first, but so many difficulties rise in my way when I come to reflect seriously, that, one after another, all have been abandoned."

" Have you heard whether any account has been given of this shipwreck in the newspapers ?" inquired Mr. Capel, who seemed as much perplexed as his friend.

" There was a paragraph in one that I saw this morning," replied the other, " but it merely mentions the fact, and regrets the inability of the editor to give either the name of the ship or the port from whence she sailed."

See page 24.

"And has no part of the wreck been picked up, by which a clue might be afforded ?"

"Not the smallest particle," answered Mr. Dawson; "even the boats went down, and thus I fear all hopes of ascertaining the truth are at an end."

"In that case," interposed Mrs. Capel, "I would send a paragraph to some of the papers, describing what took place on the night of the storm, and detailing every circumstance that might serve for the identification of the child. Her clothes, as well as those of the woman who perished, might also be described, and perhaps it might come under the notice of some one that would be able to afford the requisite information."

"I have thought of doing so," replied Mr. Dawson; "but it seems almost useless, since the notice would appear in our English newspapers, and most likely would never reach those who alone could afford us the information needed."

"Well, then," exclaimed Mr. Capel, "I think I should leave everything to chance. The infant is in good hands; and since there can be very little doubt that all its friends perished on that fatal night, you would only be giving yourself a great deal of trouble without the probability of a favourable result."

"But how," asked Mr. Dawson, "can I excuse myself to the girl when she grows up, and I relate the narrative of that fearful event which placed her under my care? Will she not think me negligent, for not having used every means in my power to discover whether she had any friends alive at the period when the ship was lost?"

"It is hardly to be expected that she will reproach you on that account," returned his friend; "and the more particularly as I have no doubt you will act towards her the part of a kind and attentive parent. Let us hope she will be grateful, and return your well-meant benevolence with thankfulness."

"I have no fear of that," replied Mr. Dawson; "and, to tell you the truth, it is the reproach of my own conscience that I fear more than anything else. Surely some plan might be thought of, by which it might be ascertained that a ship sailed on a particular day, which there is reason to believe is lost. Should I gather as much information as that, I could soon learn whether any people were on board, having a child with them of the age and appearance of our little Julia."

"Pray," inquired Mrs. Capel, "were the clothes worn by the child of good or inferior quality?"

"They were such," replied Mr. Dawson, "as you might expect to find worn by those belonging to the higher classes of life. They have, however, been carefully laid by, in hopes that some day or other they may be the means of leading to the perfect clearing up of this mystery."

"Which, in my opinion," said Mrs. Capel, "will never take place; and therefore I think whatever pains you take will be thrown away."

"Would you advise me, then, to take no steps towards tracing out the child's friends?"

"I would not do so," she replied, "unless I thought it would be labour in vain."

"The fact is," interposed her husband, addressing himself to Mr. Dawson, "she sees no chance of succeeding in the business, and would spare you the inconvenience of throwing away your time and trouble. The child is happy and comfortable enough where she is; and, as she is never likely to miss the care of her parents, it would, perhaps, be better not to let her know how she came to be thrown under your protection, till she is old enough to understand the situation in which she has been placed."

"And will it not be natural," asked Mr. Dawson, "that her first question should be to learn whether I have made any inquiry to find out who are her friends?"

"Why, no doubt she will ask that question," replied the other. "A very little explanation, however, will serve to convince her that all inquiries would have been unavailing."

"But," observed Mr. Dawson, "I have not yet taken any steps to make it known that a child has been saved from the wreck."

"And perhaps if you did," said his friend, "it would be without the desired effect. Had you indeed found a casket of valuable jewels, or a bag full of gold, I should undoubtedly have advised you to make it known as publicly as possible, in order that the property might be restored to its real owner. But here the case is widely different, for there is no doubt, though the child has been saved, her parents have perished in the ship that now lies buried at the bottom of the ocean."

"Still she may have other relatives."

"Aye, but distant ones, most likely, who would rather never hear anything more of her."

"Yet supposing there should be property?"

"In that case they would never communicate with you upon the subject, in order that they might quietly enjoy the property that ought to be hers," answered Mr. Capel. "Or perhaps she may have some hard-hearted relative, who would be glad to lay hands on the poor child, in order to put her into a nunnery, where she might pass the remainder of her days, whilst her wealth goes to enrich those who have no claim to it."

"Your argument," observed Mr. Dawson, "is hardly of sufficient weight to convince me that I ought to let the affair rest where it is."

"I presume you do not wish her to be taken away from you?"

"Certainly not," answered the other; "but if, as I imagine, she is the child of wealthy parents, should not everything be done towards assisting her to obtain possession of her own?"

"No harm can be done by a little delay," replied Mr. Capel. "Whilst under your protection she will want for nothing, and by remaining quiet for a time, something may turn up unexpectedly to bring everything to light. Such, at least, is the course I should pursue, and having stated my opinion upon the subject, I leave you to accept or reject my advice according as you may think proper. Riches will not make the child happier, and if a proof be wanting of the utter worthlessless of money beyond our necessities, look at Squire Oakley, who, with all he possesses, is perhaps the most unhappy man of our acquaintance."

"True; but that is in a great measure through his own fault."

"Aye, he would like to squander away every farthing of his possessions rather than leave it to his next heir. What but money has made him unhappy? Had he been a poor man, and obliged to earn his daily bread, he might have been in a more enviable situation."

"Well," exclaimed Mr. Dawson, "since I came here to ask your counsel, I will not reject it without consideration. For a time, at any rate, I will content myself with merely looking through the papers to see if anything is said about this shipwreck, and those who happened to be in the ill-fated vessel. Something or other may appear in the course of a short time, and if it does, I will spare neither trouble nor expense to restore the child to those who are perhaps sorrowing for her loss."

"Upon my word," exclaimed Mr. Capel, "it seems as if you were anxious to get rid of your charge as soon as you have found her."

"Better that she should be claimed now," replied Mr. Dawson, "than when she becomes more endeared to us, as she grows older. Even in the brief time that she has been with us, I love her as if she were my own child."

"Aye," interposed Mr. Capel, "that is most likely, in consequence of having fortunately been the means of saving her life. It of course increases your interest in the child, and of course as she grows older, and appreciates your kindness, she will gain still further upon your love by manifesting the gratitude she feels for the many benefits bestowed on her."

"But her gratitude will be greatly diminished," returned Mr. Dawson, "when she finds that I have taken no steps to discover from whence she came, or to whom she belongs. Really something ought to be done, or I shall rather merit her curses than her gratitude."

"Well," exclaimed the other, "if you know of any method to find out this mystery, pursue it, by all means. There is a great deal of justice in your remarks, and I know it is your most anxious desire to act for the best in the child's behalf. I also would gladly assist in restoring her to those who can substantiate a claim; but to confess the truth I see no possible means of doing so at present."

"I shall let matters remain as they are for a time," said Mr. Dawson, "and will hereafter shape out my course accordingly. Something or other may turn up in the meanwhile, and if it does, I shall then be able to act accordingly."

"That's exactly the view I take of it," replied the other. "The child will be none the worse for remaining under the protection of yourself and Miss Isabel Dawson, and as she grows older, she will make a nice little companion for my pupil, Master Frank. The young dog often complains that he has no sisters, as most of the other boys have, and now one seems to have been given him by the tempest."

" She is indeed an Ocean Child," exclaimed Mr. Dawson, " who, like Venus, was given us by the sea. In beauty the heathen goddess scarcely surpassed her, but in all else I trust our little Julia will be as much unlike her as possible."

" She will at least have the advantage of a virtuous example, both in yourself and Miss Isabel," returned Mr. Capel. " In fact, great as have been the misfortunes of this poor infant in the very outset of life, she has been so far lucky as to fall under the protection of friends, whose chief care will be to guard her from further harm."

Mr. Dawson now took leave of his friends, and bidding little Frank good-bye, mounted his horse to return home. But his mind was still far from being settled on the point to which all his thoughts were directed; the task thus imposed upon him presented new difficulties at every turn, and the more he reflected upon the subject the farther he appeared to be from arriving at a satisfactory conclusion.

A week or two after this Mr. Oakley called upon him at the vicarage, and appeared very anxious to possess himself with all the particulars relating to the finding of Julia, and the unfortunate woman who had perished on the beach. Mr. Dawson narrated everything with as much minuteness as he could, and when the squire was satisfied, he insisted upon Mr. Dawson accepting a hundred pound note towards defraying the increased charges that she would occasion in the family. It was in vain that the clergyman resisted the generous offer, for Mr. Oakley was resolute in his determination, and having thrown the pocket-book containing the money on the table, he hurried away.

It is not our intention, however, to describe all the events connected with the earliest years of our heroine. It is sufficient to say that the most careful attention was paid to her education, and that she grew in beauty and intelligence beneath the fostering care of her protectors. We may now pass over the next twelve years, during which time no tidings were heard of her relatives.

CHAPTER V.

THE SECRET DISCLOSED.

AFTER the lapse of years referred to at the conclusion of the last chapter, Frank Dawson was removed to the University of Oxford, where it was intended he should complete his studies in accordance with the plans laid down by Mr. Oakley. Even from the very first he and little Julia had been prodigious favourites with each other, and as they grew older it was remarked that they were never so happy as when together. When at school he saved all his money to purchase presents for her against he went home for the holidays, and now that he had arrived at the distinction of being a collegian he was still as thoughtful of her as ever, the only difference being that these marks of his regard were of a more costly character, and such as he knew would suit the studies to which she was devoting her attention.

On the other hand, Julia was rapidly improving under the careful instruction that was bestowed upon her by the generous benefactors whose interest in her behalf had never diminished from the moment when she had been thrown on their protection. In such society her life could not fail to be a happy one, for she was a general favourite with all who were admitted to partake of the hospitalities of the vicarage, and, occasionally, she was allowed to make visits of two or three weeks at a time to those who enjoyed the confidence and esteem of Mr. Dawson.

Thus happily passed her life till the fifteenth anniversary of her preservation from shipwreck, and though every possible exertion had been made to discover her relatives, yet the effort proved abortive, and it now began to appear pretty certain that the veil of mystery would never be removed. Fearing to trust so young a child with the secret of her first introduction to the family in which she was domesticated, Mr. Dawson had particularly requested that no one would ever throw out a hint to her upon the subject. Now, however, he thought it right that she should be made acquainted with the facts, and desiring her to follow him into the study, he cautiously disclosed the circumstances attending the fatal storm, at the same time expressing it as his opinion that all who were nearest and dearest to her had perished when the ship foundered and went to the bottom. Julia listened to him with clasped hands and quivering lips; all power of utterance seemed to have forsaken her, and it was not till a flood of tears came to her relief that she could exclaim, in broken accents,—

" Were all snatched from me—father —mother—all lost—all the prey of that fearful tempest ?"

" Alas !" cried Mr. Dawson, " there can be no doubt of it. During the interval that has intervened I have tried every means to discover the name of the vessel in the hope that I might then learn the names of those who were on board. Strange to say, however, nothing was ever mentioned of the lost ship, and, after the lapse of all these years, we seem to be as far from making the much-desired discovery as ever."

" Would that I had perished with them !" sighed Julia, in accents of despair.

" Nay," answered her protector, reproachfully; " it is your duty rather to be grateful for the life which has been spared when so many others were sacrificed."

" Pardon me," she cried, " for, indeed, sir, I scarcely know what I say. My heart is weighed down with this deep affliction, and I almost wish you had never divulged a secret of such dreadful import."

" Nothing but an imperative duty would ever have induced me to do so," answered Mr. Dawson. "To have deceived you on a subject of such vital importance would have been criminal; and, therefore, as the lesser evil, I have made you acquainted with the fact, though at the hazard of inflicting upon your heart a pang that I would have gladly spared."

" What happiness has your narrative destroyed !" cried Julia. " Till this moment I believed myself your child—that Frank was my brother. But now despair fills my heart—for those who gave me being have long since perished, and I am deprived even of the consolation of calling you by the endearing name of a father !"

" No, no, my dearest Julia !" exclaimed the clergyman, clasping her fondly to his breast; " as a parent you have ever known me, and if you now regard me in any other light, I shall, indeed, have cause to regret the moment in which I revealed to you the story of your earliest grief."

" May I," cried Julia—"may I indeed continue to call you by the sacred name of father ?"

" If you still love me you will call me by no other name," answered Mr. Dawson. " It has from the first been my special care that you should never experience the want of a parent's love, and it shall be my endeavour to prove that my affection for you is not less than parental. Had there been any possibility of avoiding it I would have spared you the pang occasioned by this discovery; but my heart told me that it must be done, and at length, though sorely against my will, I have found courage to pronounce the melancholy recital."

" Melancholy indeed," sighed Julia; " but tell me, dear father, since you still allow me to call you so, do you think there is no chance that our inquiries may lead to the discovery of my parents ?"

" I fear not," he replied—"in fact, there can be no doubt that they were on board the vessel when she sank. However, the inquiries shall be continued, and when your affliction is somewhat composed we will consult further upon this subject in order to see if something may not yet be thought of to direct us in an inquiry that has hitherto been unavailing. At any rate you may have friends or relations on the continent who will be rejoiced to hear that one whom they had given up for lost has been rescued from the fate which befell so many others."

" Had they indeed cared for me," returned Julia, " I should think they would, ere now, have found means to discover whether any part of the family escaped on the fearful night you speak of."

" I have myself argued somewhat in the same way," answered Mr. Dawson ; " and yet it is perhaps unjust to do so, since they may have pursued their inquiries with the same want of success that has attended my own exertions. Nay, I will now confess to you my selfishness, Julia ; I have almost dreaded hearing from them lest they should demand you from me, and thus bring sorrow and despair upon one who cannot part from you without enduring a pang that will go near to break his heart."

" And why should I leave you ?" she asked. " Is it not to your care that I owe my existence ? Your love has ever been to me as that of a father for his child, and no one, except a parent, shall induce me to leave the beloved home of my childhood."

" You forget," said Mr. Dawson, mildly, " that in the event of any relatives being discovered I should have no authority to refuse their demands. If they insist upon your being restored to them I must of necessity comply without hesitation."

" Then let no further inquiry be made on the subject," cried Julia. " Here I have been happy from my earliest childhood—to your generous care I owe all the blessings of life, and never will I quit the scenes which hourly remind me of the gratitude due to my excellent benefactor."

" This is indeed a noble reward for all the anxiety I have endured in your behalf," exclaimed Mr. Dawson, as he again folded her in his arms. " I was in some degree prepared to hear this avowal of filial affection, but you have even exceeded the expectation I had formed. We will still, however, endeavour to learn tidings respecting those relatives who may yet survive ; and should we succeed in discovering them, I will make a bargain to have you still an inmate of my house. There are few, I should imagine, who would hesitate to grant such a request ; and, if they insist upon taking you from me, I shall give up my vicarage as soon as Frank is able to succeed me, and take a cottage as near as possible to whatever place it may be your destiny to reside in."

" Yet had there been any relatives who cared for me," cried Julia, " one would imagine that their efforts would have succeeded before now in tracing me to this spot. They must have heard where the ship was lost, and a little inquiry would have brought them to this spot."

" You are mistaken, my dear child," answered her benefactor ; " for if, as I believe, no other life than your own was saved, it is impossible for them to obtain any clue to the precise spot where the vessel was lost. Even we, who were watching the ship from the beach, were unable to discover to what country she belonged : and though the unfortunate woman who was washed ashore with you uttered a few broken sentences, there were none present who understood the language in which she addressed herself to them."

" Were not you present ?" asked Julia.

" I was near at hand," replied Mr. Dawson ; " but amidst the howling of that dreadful tempest, it was impossible to hear the feeble words that were uttered by the expiring woman. Would to Heaven they had reached me, for it is likely they would have conveyed information of the utmost importance."

" They might indeed," sighed our heroine ; " her last words might have been intended to tell who I was, and whether my parents were in the devoted ship."

" At first," said the clergyman, " I thought the hapless creature who thus sadly perished, was your mother. My sister, however, was of a contrary opinion, and I was thus left in a more painful state of doubt than ever. She might have been your nurse, probably ; but let her have been who she may, it is evident she regarded you with the strongest affection, since it was with no little difficulty that we could release you from the convulsive grasp with which she held her little treasure."

" And, perhaps," exclaimed Julia, " it was the affectionate anxiety she felt in my behalf that led to her own untimely death."

" It is, indeed, likely enough," replied Mr. Dawson ; " for, as she contrived to reach the shore, when encumbered with her young charge, it is extremely probable that she would have survived the storm had her arms been at perfect freedom.

However, the poor creature perished, and a few days afterwards we laid her in the chancel, where a small tablet records the day of her death, and the melancholy event that led to it."

They were now interrupted by an announcement that breakfast was ready; and no sooner had Julia taken her seat at the table than Miss Isabel Dawson observed that she had been weeping. In an instant all the good lady's commiseration was exerted in behalf of her young favourite, and, casting a reproachful glance at her brother, she exclaimed,—

"I declare if I didn't think there was mischief going on when I heard that you must needs be talking to her in secret in your study. I'll be bound you have been telling her a rare rigmarole about what had better never have been mentioned; and now the end of it will be that the poor, dear child never again knows what it is to be happy."

"Tut, tut, sister," retorted Mr. Dawson; "the evil hour could not be postponed for ever; and as Julia is now old enough to be intrusted with a secret that is of so much importance to her, I thought a better opportunity for that purpose could not present itself than the anniversary of the event which threw her under our protection."

"And a very fine thing you have made of it," retorted Miss Isabel, whose temper did not much improve with her increasing years. "Her eyes are quite red with weeping, and I dare say we shall not see her smile again for this many a long day."

"Nay, dear aunt," cried Julia, addressing her, as she had always been accustomed to do, "I am not so unhappy as you imagine, though it must be confessed I could not help shedding tears when I heard the narrative of that fearful night."

"Where was the use, my dear, of your being told anything about it?" asked Miss Isabel. "You were happy enough in your ignorance, and you should have remained so if I could have had my own way in the affair. Last night I could not help remarking how happy you were, and now this morning you are as downcast as if all the care of the world were upon your shoulders. My brother, I suppose, sets himself up for a sensible man, but, in my opinion, he would have shown a great deal more sense if he had held his tongue, instead of telling you a parcel of things that there was no occasion for you to hear."

"Had I thought there was no occasion for her to hear it," exclaimed Mr. Dawson, a little put out by his sister's volubility, "I should not have afflicted her with a history so full of melancholy recollections. I, however, regarded it as a duty that must be performed, and I am sure Julia will acquit me of any intention to afflict her with unnecessary pain."

"Indeed, indeed," cried our heroine, "I am much beholden to you for the kind way in which you broke this sad story to me. It is true I could not forbear weeping at times, but the tears relieved me, and after a little time I shall quite recover myself."

"Well, my dear," said the spinster, "so that you don't give way too much to your feelings, I shall not mind; but I could never see the use of telling dismal stories, and if my brother had only taken my advice, he would have left the recital till it was ascertained whether there was any chance of anything being heard of your relatives, if indeed there should happen to be any of them alive."

"Pray, may I ask," said the vicar, "to what source you attribute Julia's grief?"

"Why, to disappointment, to be sure," replied the old lady. "She now knows herself to be an orphan, under the protection of people in very middling circumstances, when, if she gives the affair any reflection, she must be satisfied in her own mind that the parents she has lost were people belonging to the very highest rank of life."

"Indeed, my dear madam," cried Julia, earnestly, "you wrong me by such a thought. Neither riches nor rank are objects of my regard. The station in life held by my parents is a matter that I should not regard, if I could only b—— ——tain of the fate that has befallen them. At present, everything respecting the—— ——volved in darkness and mystery. If they were on board the vessel which sank, there can be no doubt that they went down with it; but if the contrary was the fact, they may yet survive to mourn the loss of a child who, they have too much reason to believe, shared the fate of the vessel which was to bear her across the treacherous ocean."

"Do not delude yourself, Julia, with a hope that they were not in the ship," said Mr. Dawson. "You were then but a few weeks old, and that circumstance alone is sufficient to convince me that they would not have trusted you to go a voyage unless they accompanied you. I well remember the night, and from the dreadful shrieks that reached us ashore, there is every certainty that a number of females were on board, and, doubtless, your poor mother was among them."

"Upon my word, you seem determined to break the poor girl's heart!" exclaimed Miss Isabel. "As if you couldn't hold your tongue and let her hope that matters will turn out better than you expect."

"Hope deferred maketh the heart sick," returned the vicar; "and I don't feel inclined to fill her heart with anticipations that can only end in disappointment. Julia, I dare say, understands the feeling with which I speak my mind thus freely, and I dare say she will give me credit for better intentions than you seem inclined to do."

"I have received too much kindness from both of you," cried Julia, "to encourage a thought that you would say or do anything to occasion me a moment's uneasiness. For my own part, too, I can see but too plainly that the chances are all against those whose parental affection I never knew, and it would only be adding to my own tortures were I to indulge in hopes that sooner or later must be destroyed."

"That, I can assure you, is exactly the light in which I view it," said Mr. Dawson.

"Well, well," cried the old lady, "so that the dear child don't fret herself into a serious fit of illness, I care nothing at all about it. But I couldn't bear to see her when she came into the room just now, looking as if you had almost broken her heart with your doleful stories."

Mr. Dawson made no further reply, but breakfast being ended, he rose from his seat and left the room. Miss Isabel now thought to have it all her own way, but our heroine wished to avoid all further dissension upon the subject; and thinking to change it, she asked he old lady if she might be permitted to see the clothes in which she had been dressed on the memorable night of the storm. This Miss Isabel would have resisted, but our heroine became more importunate in her request, and at length the box was produced in which were contained all the things which had been saved, with a view to their serving as evidence should matters take a favourable turn at any future period.

Julia shed tears of heartfelt sorrow as she gazed upon the relics which she knew had at one period belonged to those whom she now mourned as dead. They seemed to bring her back into the presence of her parents, and so completely did she lose herself in the mazes of imagination that her benefactress spoke three or four times without receiving any reply.

"Ah! I thought how it would be," she exclaimed; "these things fill your mind with all sorts of fancies, and I must have been almost as bad as my brother to show you that which I might have been certain would make you more unhappy than ever."

"It was my own wish," cried Julia; "and therefore my kind friend can have nothing to reproach herself with. These memorials occasion a momentary pang, but you may rest assured that I shall receive a consolation from beholding them, greater far than you imagine."

"Well, to be sure there is something in looking at the clothes that you wore on the night when you had so nearly been lost," said Miss Isabel. "I have often taken a sly peep at them myself when nobody was near, and somehow they made me as melancholy as I was at the moment when my brother brought you home, and popped you, dripping wet as you were, into my arms."

"I must have been a sad plague to you, I fear," exclaimed Julia, trying to divert the current of her thoughts. "And yet," she added, "I have little cause to say so, for your conduct towards me has been marked with constant kindness and affection."

"Ah, my love," exclaimed the old lady, "who could help loving you, considering the circumstances under which you were thrown under our charge? A poor, helpless orphan—herself scarcely escaping the same fate that had destroyed her parents—surely had some claim to the pity of those who had shelter to bestow."

See page 6.

"What gratitude can ever repay the benefits I have received from my first becoming an inmate of your house?" cried our heroine.

"Well," retorted Miss Isabel; "and as we have always found you grateful, we have been rewarded as much as we have any right to expect. My brother said when he first brought you into the house, that he was sure you would prove a comfort to us, and I have seen cause to acknowledge that he was right many a time when I should have been dull, but for your prattle when you first began to talk."

"And was I never troublesome?" asked Julia, smiling at the good old lady's enthusiasm.

"It is impossible for those we love to be troublesome," replied Miss Isabel. "At least, we don't think them so, and that's all the same thing. To be sure, when Frank came home for his holidays, you used to have rare romps together, and sometimes I thought the house would be turned out of windows; but my brother never complained of the noise, though I am sure it must have disturbed him when he was in the midst of his studies."

"There!" cried Julia; "I thought I must have been an annoyance to you both, sometimes."

"If people can't put up with the frolic and fun of children they are to be pitied," returned Miss Isabel. "They are not expected to be as demure as so many old men and women, for Heaven knows if they don't enjoy themselves when young, there's little chance of their doing so in after life, when the cares and anxieties of life begin."

"Yet those who are older do not always feel disposed to endure the inconvenience of seeing their house turned into a bear-garden," observed Julia.

"That is for the want of reflecting that they have ever been young themselves," replied Miss Isabel. "For my own part, I am no advocate for rudeness in children, but we must conform a little to their ways, and if people would only do that, there would not be so many fidgetty people in the world."

Julia now seemed to be absorbed in thought, and at length, once more addressing herself to her benefactress, she said,—

"Has nothing, in all these years, occurred that might throw a light upon the circumstances which so greatly concern myself?"

"We have heard absolutely nothing," replied the old lady. "My brother was constantly poring over the papers, and making inquiries of everybody that he thought could throw any light upon it, but all was of no use, and at length the thing began to die away of its own accord."

"'Tis strange," said Julia, "that no tidings should have been heard of a missing vessel. One would have thought the news must have been spread abroad, and yet no one seems to have obtained any intelligence respecting it."

"I have often wondered at the same thing myself," exclaimed Miss Isabel. "'Tis indeed strange, yet no less strange than true; and now, as the time has so long passed by, I suppose the mystery will never be removed. However, you have got a good home over your head, my dear, and there are at least two people in the world that love you, so keep a good heart, and matters won't turn out so very bad after all."

Before Julia could reply, Mr. Dawson came to invite her to take a stroll with him, which being readily acceded to, she was soon attired for walking, and, having left the house, they strolled towards that part of the beach where the shipwreck had occurred.

CHAPTER VI.

AN ADVENTURE.

THE scene thus presented to Julia, painfully reminded her of all the most appalling features belonging to the harrowing narration of her preservation from shipwreck. In imagination, she could picture every incident connected with the coast, and tears of silent agony rolled down her cheeks as she thought of the maddening terrors of her parents at the moment when a dreadful fate was about to sever them for ever. Mr. Dawson observed her grief, and, in the mildest accents of pity, sought to turn her thoughts from so painful a subject.

"I shall regain my spirits presently," she said, with an effort to appear more cheerful than she really was. "For a time, I am sure you will pardon this tribute to the memory of those whose tender care has been denied me."

"These feelings do honour to your heart," replied Mr. Dawson; "so do not believe, my dear Julia, that I have any intention of reproaching you. I would merely vert your thoughts from a painful reflection, and see you once more the happy, joyous girl that you were before I revealed the secret which preys thus heavily upon your heart."

"Believe me, dear sir," cried Julia, "I will exert myself to the utmost to overcome the grief occasioned by the severe trial it has been my lot to endure. Your kindness I can never forget, and the recollection of the inestimable benefits conferred upon me will do more than anything else to awaken me to a sense of the gratitude due to those who preserved the orphan from the misery to which she would otherwise have been doomed. Your house has been to me a happy home, but, oh! how different might have been my lot had chance, on that fatal night, thrown me under the protection of other persons."

"I can take but small credit to myself for an act of common humanity," replied her benefactor. "That which I did for you I would have done for anybody else had my assistance been required, and my chief consolation is, that you became as a daughter to me, instead of falling under the protection of some poorer person, who, unable to support the extra charge thus imposed upon him, might have been compelled to place you in the workhouse."

"And thus," cried our heroine, "my life would have been passed in poverty and degradation. The gratitude I owe you, can never, I fear, be repaid by any feeble effort of my own."

"Your love, dear child, is more than a sufficient return for the benefits conferred on me," answered Mr. Dawson. "I have ever rejoiced to see you happy, and now the greatest consolation that can be afforded me, will be to find that you have fortitude enough to conquer the grief that my narrative has occasioned."

"You shall not find me disobedient," returned Julia, with a faint effort to smile.

"I was certain of your ready acquiescence," replied her protector; "so now tell me if there is anything lying within my power, by which you may be made to forget the sorrows which have so suddenly found a way to your heart. The Stanleys have often pressed you to pay them a visit for a few weeks, and perhaps were you to do so, the change of scene and society might serve to divert your attention from the thoughts that just now afflict your mind."

"Ah, urge me not to quit my beloved home, I beseech you," cried Julia, with emotion. "In this place, I have hitherto passed my life in the possession of every enjoyment, and were I to leave it—though but for a short time—I should be most unhappy."

"Well, my love, I will not urge it," replied Mr. Dawson. "The suggestion was offered only that you might make your choice, and believe me your departure from the vicarage would have occasioned me more sorrow than you are aware of."

"Can sorrow," asked our heroine, "ever reach a heart so kind and gentle as yours?"

"I am a prey to heavier griefs than I permit the world to know of," replied Mr. Dawson, while his voice trembled with emotion. "For years I have endured them in secret, passing the night in sleepless anxiety, and rising each morning unrefreshed, though I have had sufficient command over myself to conceal my grief from those who would also have been made unhappy by becoming participators."

"Surely," cried Julia, "my benefactor can have no enemies to destroy his peace?"

"In good time you shall be made acquainted with my sad story," answered the vicar. "To you I can trust it safely, and, perhaps, my heart may feel relieved when it is unburdened of the heavy load with which it has been so long borne down."

"Would it not be better to relieve yourself at once?" suggested Julia; "we are here alone, and, perhaps, in listening to your sorrows, I may forget those which oppress my own bosom."

"At this moment I feel myself unequal to the task," replied her guardian. "Besides, I require some little preparation before I can properly connect the events it is my intention to narrate. I will endeavour to recollect the incidents, and, perhaps, to-morrow, I will take an opportunity to give you the recital."

" Would that it were in my power to heal the wound that sorrow has made in your heart," cried Julia, earnestly. " Till now, I never guessed that an affliction preyed upon your mind, and already have I half forgotten my own woes in thinking of the far greater ones that harass my generous benefactor."

" Let me entreat you not to surmise anything till you have heard the story from my own lips," said Mr. Dawson. " You cannot guess what it is that has embittered so great a portion of my life; and, therefore, it will be better to await with patience the moment when I can reveal all."

" Is your sister acquainted with it ?" asked Julia.

" Only slightly," he replied; " and, as years have passed away, it is probable the circumstance has ceased to occupy a place in her memory. Besides, I have always been careful to appear cheerful and unconstrained in her society; so that it is to be hoped she has not observed that the cankerworm of grief is gnawing at my heart even at those moments when I endeavour to appear most at ease."

" You have excited my curiosity," exclaimed our heroine, " and most anxiously shall I look forward to the moment when you may find it convenient to redeem the pledge you have given."

" I promise you shall not be kept long in suspense," replied the vicar. " But we will now prepare to return home, Julia, and, if you please, we will take the church in our way, and I will then show you the humble memorial placed there to record the melancholy fate of the unfortunate woman who perished on the night that gave you to my care."

Julia readily assented to this proposition, and, leaving the sea-shore, they proceeded across some fields that lie towards the same sacred edifice which was the object of their visit. The conversation of Mr. Dawson became somewhat more varied, now that he had quitted the topic upon which he had been speaking, and our heroine, perceiving that his spirits were growing lighter, forbore to speak further upon a subject that evidently afforded him a great deal of anxiety.

" I think," he said, at last, " my sister told me that you had received a letter from Frank; does he speak of coming to spend the vacation at the vicarage ?"

" That seems to have been the sole object of his letter," replied Julia.

" Does he speak of nothing else ?"

" Oh, yes," she replied, " he says much about the pleasure he anticipates in seeing you and his aunt, both of whom, he tells me, are scarcely ever out of his mind for half-an-hour together."

" And is there no one else who he is anxious to see ?" asked the vicar, with an expressive smile.

" Oh, yes," she replied, blushing as she saw the good man's eyes intently fixed upon her. " I believe he will not be sorry to meet me, for we have been such old playfellows, you know, that it is quite natural we should think of each other sometimes."

" Quite natural, indeed," said the vicar, thoughtfully; " and, I suppose, if the truth was known, he has told you how eagerly he looks forward to the moment that will release him from the restraint of college, and permits his immediate return home."

" He seems more anxious than ever to see us," answered our heroine; " indeed, he speaks of hardly anything else but the pleasant walks he and I are to have together; and then he tells me, too, that he has been learning to play the flute, in order that he may accompany me when I sit down to the piano. Is it not very thoughtful of him, my dear sir, to take so much trouble, merely to oblige me ?"

" Very," replied the vicar, drily; " but I have always observed, Julia, that you were an especial favourite of his, even from your earliest infancy."

" That was natural enough," said our heroine, " since we were playmates together, and regarded each other as brother and sister. Would to Heaven that I had never heard your narrative, my kind benefactor, since I can no longer look upon Frank in the same light that I used to do."

" Why, surely you will not love him less ?"

"No," she replied; "but there cannot be the same affection that there was. I must be more distant and reserved towards him, and that, I am sure, will vex him more than anything else I could do."

"Let there be no change in the feelings with which you have ever regarded each other," replied the vicar, earnestly. "Frank is an excellent youth, who deserves the high estimation in which you hold him; and you, also, merit the affection of his warm and honourable heart. As brother and sister you have loved each other, and now that you are aware no affinity exists between you, I can see no reason why that feeling of tenderness should be effaced from your hearts."

"I am sure," cried Julia, artlessly, "it would be from no wish of my own."

"Then I think I can answer for Frank," returned Mr. Dawson. "He possesses a fine, generous disposition, and deep would be his grief should there be any perceptible change in your manner towards him."

"There shall be none," exclaimed Julia; "beneath your watchful eye there can be no harm in continuing towards each other as we always have been, and I think Aunt Isabel, as I must still continue to call her, would never forgive me if, by coldness towards her favourite, I should cause him a moment's uneasiness."

"You have exactly guessed the feeling with which she would regard her nephew's chagrin," replied Mr. Dawson. "I myself hardly ever dared to correct him even when he was a child, unless, indeed, I thought proper to run the risk of being called a cruel and unnatural father. She has always been over-indulgent to him, and it has often been a source of gratification to me that he has not been entirely spoiled by the extraordinary partiality she has manifested toward him."

"That, perhaps, is owing to his own good sense," replied our heroine, who was always among the first to put in a good word for Frank Dawson.

"It must be acknowledged, he is no fool," answered the father, gratified with her remark. "Frank never yet occasioned me an uneasy moment, and it is the confidence I repose in him that makes me wish you to continue on the same terms as when you believed him to be your brother."

"But, of course," said Julia, "you will no longer conceal from him the real position in which we stand towards each other?"

"I should rather think he must know something about it already," replied Mr. Dawson. "At all events, it is likely enough my sister has told him the story of your discovery on the beach, though under a strict charge never to mention it to you or anybody else, till he found that it was no longer a secret."

"Yet, if that had been the case," observed our heroine, "I should think he could hardly have helped forgetting himself in some of our interviews. To the present time he always calls me his sister, and his manner, more than anything else, convinces me that he knows nothing of the shipwreck that threw me, a helpless orphan, on the charity and protection of strangers."

"You think, then, my sister has been prudent enough to keep her counsel?"

"Such is certainly my impression."

"Well, I hope it may be so," answered her guardian; "because, if she has mentioned it to one person, she may have done so to others. The story, of course, was well known throughout the neighbourhood at the time when the affair occurred; but, like other nine days' wonders, it gradually ceased to be thought of, and it is now long since I have heard any one speak of you except as my daughter. But we have now arrived at our place of destination," he added, as they entered the church porch, and, leading her up to the chancel, he pointed out a plain-looking tablet against the wall, which Julia, till that moment, had never taken any particular notice of.

"That," he said, slightly agitated, "is the only memorial that has been raised to her who lost her own life in a generous attempt to save yours. It was placed there within a few months after she had been laid in the tomb, and, as you see, the brief inscription upon it records the day of her death, and the fatal accident which threw her upon our shores to perish."

"Were no letters or papers found upon her to prove who she was, or from where she came?"

"Unfortunately, there was not a memorandum in her pocket," replied Mr. Dawson. "Had there been but a few lines it might have served as a clue to lead us to more important discoveries. You have seen all the relics which we have carefully preserved, and, judging from the missal which was found upon her, I have thought that, in all probability, she was a native of some country where the Roman Catholic religion predominates."

"Were no other bodies washed upon any part of the coast?" asked Julia.

"I never heard of any," he replied, "though I made anxious inquiries for many weeks afterwards, and even offered a large reward to anybody who would give me information of such an event taking place, in order that I might see if papers or documents were to be found, throwing any light on this mystery."

"Then to Providence alone belongs the clearing of it up," cried Julia, after a pause. "At first, I was in hopes that all trace of the ship was not lost, but since the destruction has been so complete, both of the vessel and her luckless crew and passengers, I begin to fear that we must wait with resignation till the secret is revealed in its own good time."

"In that case," said her benefactor, "your wisest course will be to think of it as little as possible. Where all is uncertainty reflection can avail you nothing, since the only proof of your identity is in the clothes which you wore on the night we saved you from the angry waves. Should any one recognize them at a future time we may indeed hope that the reward of our long anxiety is near at hand. In the meanwhile, you will remain, as hitherto, the inmate of my humble home, which your presence has gladdened on so many occasions, when my heart would otherwise have been weighed down with despondency."

"Has it indeed been my happy lot," cried Julia, "at any time to drive from your mind the memory of past sorrows?"

"Ay, often, my dear girl," answered the vicar; "and my heart warms with gratitude towards you when I think of it."

"Then how much greater ought my gratitude to be," cried Julia, ardently, "for the inestimable favours that have been conferred on me by those who sheltered and protected a helpless stranger! Indeed, when I reflect on ——"

She was here interrupted by a quick footstep that was heard approaching up the middle aisle of the church, and when she and her benefactor turned round to discover who the intruder was, they saw a stranger of rough and unprepossessing appearance, who bowed haughtily as their eyes were directed towards him, and then advancing three or four paces nearer, he presented a letter to our heroine.

"Touch it not, Julia!" exclaimed Mr. Dawson, in a tone of alarm; and then, addressing himself to the stranger, he inquired who it was from. The man, however, made no reply; but, with an impatient gesture, he again offered it for her acceptance.

"By whom have you been sent with that letter?" demanded the vicar.

An ominous shake of the head again declared the stranger's determination not to speak, and Mr. Dawson was about to repeat the question, when the man threw the letter at the feet of Julia, and, turning quickly upon his heel, departed without deigning to utter a word.

"Of a truth this is a strange adventure," exclaimed the vicar, as soon as he could recover from his surprise. "The fellow came upon us like a ghost, and, having fulfilled his errand, departs pretty much in the same fashion. This must be inquired into, for I have a notion that his purpose in thus seeking us out is not a very good one."

"Do you know anything of the man?" asked Julia, in alarm.

"I never recollect having seen him in my life before," replied Mr. Dawson; "to be sure this place is rather dark, and the fellow seemed to screen his face from us as much as he could, so that I can hardly say for certain whether we have ever met on any previous occasion."

"His silence," observed our heroine, "makes it appear that he was afraid of speaking lest the tones of his voice should be recognized. His purpose, too, cannot be a very friendly one, or he would have taken a different way to present himself before us."

"We will soon see what motive he has in view," said Mr. Dawson, taking up the letter, which was still lying at Julia's feet. "I suppose this will give a full explanation of what he means; and, though the letter is addressed to you, I will, with your permission, make myself acquainted with its contents."

So saying, he broke open the seal, and, having hastily run his eye over the contents, read it aloud to his companion, in the following words :—

"An unknown friend takes this method of addressing Julia Dawson, to tell her that the mystery which involves her life may now be unveiled. Let her repair this evening to the abbey ruins, an hour after the moon rises, and she will meet one who will be a friend or an enemy according to the reception he may meet with."

"A strange affair, truly," exclaimed Mr. Dawson, as he finished perusing the letter. "Your unknown correspondent deals in mystery, the better, I suppose, to ensure your giving him the meeting he so modestly requests."

"Has he not signed his name ?" asked Julia.

"No; I suppose he leaves you to guess that," replied her guardian; "or, perhaps, he will tell you when the meeting takes place."

"Your tone," exclaimed our heroine, "tells me that you would persuade me against keeping the appointment."

"Indeed, would I," answered Mr. Dawson; "secresy always begets suspicion, and my own impression is, that this fellow has some bad purpose in view."

"And yet he hints," said Julia, "that he can explain matters of importance to me."

"That may only be for the purpose of prevailing on you to meet him at the abbey ruins,' answered the vicar, doubtfully.

"But, if I fail to do so," cried Julia, "may I not throw away the only chance that remains to clear up the mystery which you yourself are so anxious should be explained ?"

"It is by no means certain that this stranger can do it," answered Mr. Dawson. "If he means that which is fair and straightforward, why did he not enter into the explanation just now ? A better opportunity he could not have had, and if he had wished it I would have retired beyond ear-shot, though not far enough to lose sight of him. In short, my dear Julia, I have formed a very indifferent opinion of him, and, if you take my advice, you will remain in doors for some time, so as not to give him a chance of waylaying you again."

"And thus throw away the only opportunity I may ever have of learning secrets that are of the utmost importance to me ?"

"If I thought the interview he seeks could be of any advantage to you, I, as your friend, should be the last to say a word against it," replied the vicar. "But there is too much reason to believe that it is a trick to ensnare you, and, therefore, do I most earnestly entreat you to think no more of it."

"What if you were to accompany me ?"

"Why, that would be rather better," answered Mr. Dawson; "though I need hardly say my protection would be of little service in the event of any stratagem being intended. However, if you have really made up your mind upon the subject, I will go with you to-night to the place appointed; but mind nothing must be said to my sister, or her alarm for our safety will spoil all. Appear to be in your usual spirits, and at the proper time I will make an excuse, so that we may go out together without giving rise to any suspicion."

This arrangement having been agreed upon, they quitted the church, and took the path which led towards the vicarage. During the walk, short as it was, Julia had time to calm the agitation into which she had been thrown, and when they reached home she was as composed and cheerful as ever.

CHAPTER VII.

THE ABBEY RUINS.

FAITHFULLY did Julia keep her promise, for, whatever might be the feelings that agitated her heart, she assumed an appearance of gaiety while in the presence of Isabel, that could not fail to lull all suspicion. As evening drew on, she sat down to her harp, and enlivened her benefactors with all the airs that she knew to be their especial favourites. The old lady, who was never so happy as when she saw her protege in good spirits, could not conceal the satisfaction she felt at thus seeing her resume her usual amusements, and, smiling with her customary good-humour, she said,—

"Ah! this is just as it should be, for girls of your age, Julia, should not go moping about the house when their hearts ought to be gay and cheerful. Troubles come on thick enough as we grow older, and it's quite time to put on sorrowful looks when there is real occasion for them."

"I have profited by your good advice, my dear madam," replied Julia; "besides, it would look like ingratitude to give way to melancholy, when I know everything is done by my kind friends to make me as happy as possible."

"Well, well, my love," exclaimed Miss Isabel, "then, as that is the case, I shall not scold my brother as I intended to do for telling you about the storm that brought you to our coast. There was no occasion for you to have known anything about it these ten years to come, and indeed if the affair had been kept secret for ever, I don't know that you would have been any the worse for it. However, seeing you so cheerful again has put an end to the vexation I felt when I saw your eyes red with weeping at the story you had been listening to."

" I was a weak, foolish girl to give way to my tears, when I ought to have shown more firmness," replied Julia, with animation. "Now, however, that I have repented the folly, you shall see that I will give you no more reason to reproach me for yielding, when I ought to be firm."

" That's well said."

" I have to apologise, too," continued our heroine, " for having caused you so much uneasiness."

" Nay, you shall make no apologies to me," exclaimed the good lady, " for I am already too happy at seeing that the mischief is less than I thought for. You shall go out more frequently, Julia, and by mixing a little more in society, you will soon learn to forget all you have heard."

" Julia is likely to remain at home more than ever," said Mr. Dawson.

" And why, pray?"

" Because I think her safety requires the precaution," replied the vicar.

" Her safety requires it!" reiterated Miss Isabel; " surely you don't mean to say that any danger threatens our young favourite?"

" No, no," stammered her brother; " I scarcely meant to say so much as that; but Julia, I dare say, understood what I mean, and she will not disoblige me, I am very certain."

" Then you intend to keep her a close prisoner in the house?"

" Nay, there will be no occasion for it, since I shall always be ready to accompany her whenever she feels inclined to take a walk."

" And so she is not to stir a step, unless you go dangling after her."

" There is no occasion for me always to be her companion," replied Mr. Dawson. " You can go with her, when she is merely going to stroll about in the neighbourhood of our house."

" Upon my word, this new arrangement of yours quite puzzles me," exclaimed Miss Isabel. " One would imagine, by all this care, that somebody was going to run away with her."

" No one shall do so if I can prevent it," replied her brother; " so you will oblige me by making no more remarks on a resolution that has been formed after due consideration."

" You have heard something, then, to cause alarm, and yet I am not to be let into the secret," exclaimed the lady. " But never mind, a woman's ingenuity is not to be defeated, and depend on it I shall find all out sooner than you expect. Tell me, Julia, has anything happened to make my brother so much afraid of trusting you out of his sight. You are silent; then now I am sure there is some mischief in the wind, and I am the only person that is considered unworthy to be trusted with a secret."

See page 30

" Do not be so uncharitable as to misjudge my motives," exclaimed Mr. Dawson. " That I have some reason to apprehend danger to our young favourite you may well imagine, but the alarm may be groundless, and therefore it would be useless on my part to explain myself further at present."

The old lady was silenced by these words, but, after considering the subject a little while in her own mind, she said,—

" Pray may I inquire when your watchfulness over Julia is to commence ?"

" It has commenced already."

" Indeed ! then if she wants to take a walk out to-morrow, you will accompany her ?"

" I intend to do so this very night."

" To-night ! why, you must be crazed to think of taking her out at night."

" Not as crazed as you think, my dear sister," replied Mr. Dawson ; " the truth is, Julia, as you have heard, has frequently expressed a wish to see the cascade by moonlight. I have promised to accompany her, and to-night offers an opportunity that I cannot very well resist."

" Will you go, Julia ?" demanded Miss Isabel, between doubt and surprise.

" Certainly, my dear madam," she replied ; " since my benefactor has been kind enough to say that he will put himself so much out of the way for me."

" Really this is most incomprehensible," cried the old lady. " However, I can see plainly enough that there is some mystery in it, and if I cannot get to the bottom of it one way, I must another."

" You may spare yourself all trouble, my dear sister," exclaimed the vicar, " for if you will only have patience for a few days, I will promise to let you know the ground upon which my apprehension is founded. In the meantime you may make yourself quite easy under my assurance that Julia is not threatened with any immediate danger. I am only using a little caution, in order that we may be upon our guard in the event of any evil practices being designed."

As it was now nearly the time appointed for the meeting, Julia and her guardian took their departure from the house, and made their way towards the abbey ruins. It was a calm, quiet night, and the moon, which had already made her appearance above the row of trees that skirted the abbey grounds, added a solemnity to the scene, that communicated itself to the minds of those who had thus come forth to meet a stranger whose purposes in seeking the interview were unknown. Julia looked round her with trembling dread, yet she whispered not a word to Mr. Dawson, lest he should repent the step he had taken, and return home without accomplishing the design they contemplated. No one was yet to be seen about the place, and after waiting a quarter of an hour in the greatest anxiety, Mr. Dawson was about to suggest that they might as well retrace their steps, when the figure they had seen before in the church, rose up suddenly before them, and addressing Mr. Dawson, inquired angrily why he had intruded himself upon an interview that it was intended should be strictly private.

" The question, methinks, is scarcely necessary," returned the vicar, placidly ; " since, as the guardian of this young female, I should hardly trust her alone, and at such an hour, with a stranger whose object I am not acquainted with."

" And by what right," demanded the other, " do you claim the guardianship of this young lady ?"

" By a right which no one dares to dispute," answered Mr. Dawson, firmly. " There were no others to protect her when first she found a shelter beneath my roof, and since no one has claimed her from that time to the present, I feel as interested in her safety as if she had been my own flesh and blood."

" You have never heard, I suppose, anything of the family to which she belongs ?"

" Never."

" And have no hopes of tracing her relatives ?"

" Not the slightest."

" In that case I may, perhaps, assist you," exclaimed the stranger.

" Indeed !" cried Mr. Dawson; " aid me but in that endeavour, and I will reward you to the utmost of my means."

" Ay, with money, I suppose ?"

" Yes," replied the vicar ; " gold is the usual exchange for services performed."

" But gold is not what I covet," replied the other. " I can give you all the information you require of this girl's family, but it must be on certain conditions."

" Name them," said Mr. Dawson; " and, if not too extravagant, I promise to accede to them."

"I must have her hand in marriage."

"Nay," exclaimed the vicar, startled at the unexpected proposition, "she is too young."

"I was aware that such would be your objection," returned the other; "but, perhaps, there will no longer be an impediment in my way when I explain that I do not ask an immediate marriage with the girl, but only require your solemn pledge that she shall be mine before the expiration of five years."

"Who is it," exclaimed Mr. Dawson, "that makes so extraordinary a demand?"

"One whom you know not, but who does not hesitate to tell his name," answered the other. "I am called Jasper Hemmingsby in the neighbourhood from which I come."

"Where is that?"

"At present it is unnecessary to explain myself any further," replied the man; "you have now heard as much as I think proper to say with respect to myself, and it only remains for you to declare whether the demand I have made is to be granted."

"It has come so suddenly upon me, that I can give you no reply," exclaimed Mr. Dawson. "Besides, would it not be better to wait the expiration of the five years, and then, if I live, I shall be better prepared to give you an answer."

"In five years the girl may be married to somebody else," exclaimed Jasper; "and as that happens to be the very thing I want to prevent, I must have your promise now, or the secret I possess respecting the girl dies with me."

"Can you give me any information respecting her family?"

"I can."

"Is it noble?"

"Yes."

"Rich?"

"Ay," replied Jasper, with a sneer; "or I should not be so desirous to make one of it."

"And you would marry Julia for no other purpose than to possess yourself of the wealth that may hereafter be hers?"

"Is it not inducement enough?" demanded the other. "Besides, if I am to be rejected, she will die in the same ignorance that she has lived."

"You would punish her, then," exclaimed Mr. Dawson, "though she is not in any way to blame."

"It is not my business to consider whether it is her fault or not," answered Jasper; "you are the person that should look after her interest, and if you think proper to oppose me, why, she must take the consequences, that's all I know about it."

"Let us return home, dear sir," cried Julia, anxiously pressing the hand of her benefactor. "We have done wrong in coming to meet this stranger; but we may yet repair the error by hastening back without delay."

"Hah!" exclaimed the fellow; "so you would oppose me, too, would you? I am despised because you know me not; but beware, for I can have vengeance if I am deprived of every other satisfaction. I can deprive her of the inheritance which a word of mine would make hers; and if that is not enough to satisfy my burning hatred, I can follow her from place to place till she prays for death as the only hope that remains to escape from my persecution."

"Can you be villain enough," cried the vicar, "to meditate the persecution of one who never injured you?"

"Villain I am none," returned the other, sullenly; "though you may force me to become one if you persist in refusing to aid me in the way I have demanded."

"The orphan girl of whom you speak," returned Mr. Dawson, "has ever been as a daughter to me, and base indeed must I be to promise her to a man whose intentions I have so much reason to suspect."

"Am I scorned," exclaimed Jasper, "because my appearance is against me, or would you reject a lover for no other cause than the mystery with which it is his pleasure to envelop himself? I may be equal in rank to the girl I seek, in spite of appearances, yet am I looked upon with scorn, and my offer rejected as if I was a beggar asking for a crust to save me from starvation."

"Had you been a beggar," returned Mr. Dawson, "I could have relieved your wants without hesitating a moment to inquire whether you were worthy of the alms bestowed. But you require from me a prize of inestimable value, and rather than resign her, I will endure the consequences of your fury, however vindictive they may be."

"Then whatever follows," exclaimed the other, "will be the result of your own obstinacy. I have asked no such great favour that I am aware of; the girl is at present a beggar, depending upon the charity of those into whose hands chance has thrown her, and she will continue in ignorance of that which she might otherwise know, unless you will listen to a proposition that will be of the greatest benefit to herself."

"Oh, heed him not!" cried Julia, clinging yet closer to the arm of her protector. "Let him slay me if he will, but never again will I trust myself in the presence of one who can thus insult helpless age to gain his own vile ends."

"Be careful how you provoke me, young lady," exclaimed Jasper, threateningly, "for I am not a man that's used to be browbeaten in this way. I sought you and your friend here for a particular purpose; I have said that it is in my power to make resolutions of the greatest consequence to yourself, and have not asked anything more than Mr. Dawson's interest in my behalf till he has seen whether I can perform all I have promised. If I fail, he will not be bound to any pledge that he may make; and, if I fulfil my offer, he surely cannot object to make good the promise I got from him."

"You have heard my answer," exclaimed Mr. Dawson; "and the more I listen to you the more do I become convinced that your design is only to deceive me. I have no proof that you can perform any portion of the services you have proposed."

"But you soon can have it, if you like to put me to the test," answered the other.

"In one word—will you inform me of all the particulars relating to Julia's family?"

"Ay; upon the terms you have already heard."

"And upon no other?"

"Why should I, when there is no reason to oppose against my will?" demanded Jasper. "You can't choose a better husband, that I know of, and at any rate there's no one else that can tell you who she is, or where her relatives are to be found."

"Let me, then, for ever remain in ignorance," cried Julia; "for I can endure anything rather than again be thrown in the way of one whose presence inspires me with dread."

"This prejudice is all owing to you," exclaimed Jasper, fiercely, addressing himself to the vicar. "She would have listened to me, and a fair bargain might have been made between us, if you had not interfered. Let us speak together for a few moments, and, if my arguments do not then convince her that it would be better to accept my offer, I will pledge my word never to see her again."

"You ask me that which you know I cannot accede to," replied Mr. Dawson. "I came hither as a protector, and will not lose sight of her for a moment."

"You her protector!" exclaimed the other scornfully; "think you, then, my will is to be thwarted by a man that I could crush beneath my foot?"

"If my years cannot spare me from your violence," retorted the clergyman, "I have indeed been wasting my time upon a ruffian who deserves not the favour I have thus far shown him."

"Favour!"

"Yes; I am not so far from assistance but my voice would be heard if I thought it necessary to alarm any part of my family."

"It would answer no good end," retorted Jasper; "for, supposing the assistance you speak of should come, I could make my escape without much difficulty. Every chance was carefully weighed before I came here, and my first care was to provide for my own safety in case of treachery. I am armed and desperate, so that if an attempt should be made to capture me, whatever blood may be shed will be caused by your own rashness."

"Do you really go armed when about to ask a favour?" demanded the vicar reproachfully.

"This is no favour," answered Jasper. "I offer to do the girl a service that will prove most important, and, in return, I expect to receive what I consider a fair compensation. The information I can give is of more importance than you imagine, yet my terms are rejected with reproaches and scorn."

"The truth is," replied Mr. Dawson, "I think we can do without your assistance. Your words have roused me to fresh exertion, and I shall now institute inquiries in every direction to discover the secret that you boast can be revealed by no other person than yourself."

"Do as you please," retorted the other; "waste months, nay, years, in these inquiries, and at last you will be no nearer to the truth than at the present moment. All trace of the girl is lost; she is supposed to have perished in the storm, and the fair inheritance which might be her's, will go to others who have no just claim to it."

"I can cheerfully sacrifice all," cried Julia, "rather than be under an obligation to one who seeks to make an advantage of the secret. Hitherto I have been happy and content under the care of my generous friends, and never will I leave them, even though it might be to take possession of a rich inheritance."

"Humph! than you prefer beggary to wealth?"

"Beggary will never be her lot," answered Mr. Dawson; "though unfortunately it will not be in my power to bestow so much upon her as I could have wished. But she has other friends besides myself, and shall not be crushed by the evil practices of a villain."

"Villain in your teeth!" exclaimed Jasper furiously, and opening a clasp knife which he had snatched from his pocket, he stepped forward to plunge it into the heart of his antagonist, when loud shouts were heard close at hand. Appalled by the unexpected approach of danger, the ruffian started back, dropped the weapon from his hand, and, leaping over the wall, disappeared before any attempt could be made to secure him. Almost at the same moment, Richard Martin, the faithful servant of Mr. Dawson, made his appearance, with three or four of the neighbouring fishermen. With a shout of joy the former advanced at a quick pace, and seizing the hand of his master, exclaimed,—

"Oh, sir, how glad I am that we have found you and Miss Julia at last. There's poor missis almost out of her wits lest any mischief should have happened, and so she sent me out to look after you and my young lady."

"Have you been seeking for us anywhere else?" asked the vicar.

"Yes, sir, we went down to the cascade, because something was said just before leaving home, that you were going to show Miss Julia how pretty it looks by moonlight. Missis said she was sure we should find you there, but when we got to the place, nothing was to be seen of you, and then we came to the abbey ruins, knowing that it's often a favourite walk of yours."

"Then now hasten back, and let my sister know that we shall follow you immediately."

"Hadn't we better go with you, sir, in case of accident?" asked Richard, anxiously.

"There is nothing to be afraid of," said his master; "so make all the haste you can, and appease any alarm that may be caused by our absence."

Richard Martin could no longer hesitate, and casting a wistful glance at his master, he and his companions set forward at their utmost speed. The vicar and his fair charge immediately followed, and, in the course of their walk homewards, it was arranged that in spite of any questions that might be asked, nothing should be said about the stranger whose appearance had occasioned so much alarm.

CHAPTER VIII.

AN ALARM.

WHEN they reached the vicarage, they found Miss Isabel in a state of the greatest alarm at the long absence of Mr. Dawson and her young favourite. Richard Martin had returned and announced that they were on their way back, but the good old lady was not to be convinced by anything short of occular demonstration, and she was just about to set forth in quest of them, when the persons she sought reached home with as much apparent calmness as if nothing had occurred to disturb their serenity.

"Why, where in the name of fortune have you been all this time?" she exclaimed, half pettishly, as they entered the room. "Here have I been frightened out of my life at your long absence, and ——"

"I dare say," interrupted her brother, smiling, "you have bestowed a great deal more thought upon us than there was any occasion for. We told you where we were going to, and considering how fine the evening is, you might have guessed that we were tempted to extend it a little."

"Ah, brother!" cried Miss Isabel, "but as you are not much given to night rambling, it is not to be wondered at if I was alarmed lest anything had happened. And see how pale our poor Julia is—surely she has either been very much frightened at something, or else you have dragged her about till she is scarce able to stand."

"I dare say she is fatigued," replied Mr. Dawson, afraid of saying too much.

"Fatigued! why, she looks downright ill. Now I'll be bound, I can guess it all, you have been talking to her again about family affairs, and she's fretting herself to death, because we cannot put her in the way of finding her relatives."

"Why, it cannot be denied that something has been said on that subject," answered her brother; "but I was in hopes Julia had too much firmness to suffer a temporary disappointment to prey upon her spirits. Indeed, I am quite certain that her paleness is caused rather by fatigue than anxiety."

"Is it so?" asked the old lady.

"Believe me, dear madam," exclaimed Julia, "the little anxiety that I felt has ceased to trouble me. In my benefactors I place the greatest reliance—their kindness encourages me to hope for a favourable termination of our inquiries, and, whatever may be the result, I feel assured that while a hope remains, they will never relax in their endeavours."

"Why, that's true enough," returned the old lady; "and, for my part, I care not what trouble it may give me, so that we do but succeed in the end."

"And that we shall do, I am certain, notwithstanding the unpromising aspect of things at present. But the battle is not always to the strong, nor the race to the swift, and take my word for it, the truth will come out some time or other, when we least expect it."

"That's exactly what I have always thought of it myself," exclaimed Miss Isabel, who generally took to herself the credit of other people's ideas. "I have fancied that the mystery cannot last for ever, and as every day must bring us nearer a discovery, I begin to expect that a very little time will see the accomplishment of our wishes."

"And then perhaps she may be taken away from us," observed Mr. Dawson, in whose mind this thought was always uppermost. "It has ever been my most anxious wish that Julia may be restored to her friends, yet the desire has damped when I think of what the consequence may be."

"Can you then believe me so ungrateful as to leave the friends who sheltered and protected me, when I should otherwise have perished?" cried Julia, in accents of grief.

"I am sure, as far as your own heart is concerned, you will never be forgetful of the care we have bestowed upon you," replied the old lady. "But should you ever be claimed by those who can prove a right to your guardianship, how can any of us resist it?"

"They must be cruel, indeed," exclaimed our heroine, "to insist upon the separation of those who love each other as we do. Nay, should it come to that, I know not that I should yield even to the commands of relatives, who could exercise so tyrannical an act of authority."

"Spoken with spirit, my dear girl," cried Miss Isabel; "I like to hear it, Julia, though, between ourselves, it's hardly likely that your friends would listen to the remonstrances of one who they would consider bound to obey their commands."

"We will wait till the di covery has taken place," said Mr. Dawson, who, though silent, had been highly amused with what was going on. "At present we are talking without any immediate purpose in view, so that it would be difficult to say how we should act in such a case."

"Would you part with her without so much as remonstrating?" asked the old lady.

"Stop till we know, in the first place, whether she will be claimed," said Mr. Dawson, "and in the second, whether they will insist upon her leaving us. For my own part, I think there are few persons who would be cruel enough to insist upon a separation; nor can I believe it possible that such a thing would ever be seriously contemplated."

"Yet there are some strange people in the world," observed Miss Isabel, "and for my own part I never expect too much from any one."

"A very good rule to go by if it is not carried too far," said her brother. "In the present case we must be content to wait till the period we are speaking of arrives, and when it does, we must make the best bargain we can respecting the future disposal of Julia."

"Oh, sir!" exclaimed Richard, as he entered the room, pale and trembling; "I've had such a fright—you should have seen what I have, and ——"

"What have you seen?" demanded Mr. Dawson, with alarm.

"A man."

"What man?"

"A stranger."

"Well, is there anything so remarkable in seeing a stranger about the place?"

"No, sir," replied the domestic, "but this one was a suspicious-looking fellow, and I have a notion he is after no good."

"Where did you see him?"

"In the garden."

"Indeed! a robber perhaps."

"A robber?" screamed Miss Isabel, terrified at the bare idea of so dangerous a person being in their vicinity.

"Yes, ma'am, I rather think master's right in his guess this time," said Richard; "The fellow didn't know I was watching so near, and there I saw him trying to peep in at this window—and then he stopped and listened to what was being said. 'So,' think I, 'there's something going wrong,' and with that I crept softly towards the door, intending to raise an alarm, when the fellow heard my footsteps, I suppose, and running away as hard as he could, he was out at the back gate before I could sufficiently recover from my surprise to cry out."

"We shall all be murdered!" groaned Miss Isabel, in accents of despair.

"Nay, may dear sister," exclaimed Mr. Dawson; "do not, I beseech you, give way to this unnecessary alarm before you know whether there is any danger." Then turning towards Richard, he inquired if he was sure it was a man that he had seen in the garden.

"Quite sure," replied Richard; "what else could it have been?"

"A shadow of one of the trees cast by the moonlight across the garden," replied his master.

"It was much more like a substance," replied the domestic.

"Perhaps it may have been the person we just now saw," cried Julia, forgetting in her terror the promise she had given to be cautious.

"What man do you speak of?" cried Miss Isabel, catching eagerly at the words which had been thus heedlessly uttered.

"Merely a person that we saw in the course of our walk," replied Mr. Dawson with as much composure as he could assume. "Julia took it into her head that he was a suspicious character, and in her alarm at Richard's news, it was natural enough that her thoughts should first be directed to the person who had terrified her."

"It's very likely to be the same man," cried Miss Isabel; "and if so, you may depend upon it he is lurking about to rob the house."

"If that's the case," said Mr. Dawson, "as a matter of precaution, some of us had better sit up and watch through the night."

"Somebody had much better go and look round about the place to see if he is lurking anywhere near the house," said the old lady. "I dare say he is waiting his opportunity, and when all is quiet he will return to cut our throats and plunder the house."

"I think master's plan is the best, ma'am," exclaimed Richard, who had no wish to be sent out on such a dangerous expedition. "We can sit up here very well, and if any one should attempt to force his way in, I'll give him the contents of the blunderbuss that hangs up over the kitchen chimney."

"There must be no bloodshed," interposed Mr. Dawson. "This house should be the abode of peace, and even in self-defence, I would not take away the life of a fellow creature."

"But if a fellow creature attempt to rob us, he deserves neither pity nor compassion," said Miss Isabel. "I have no patience to hear you talk of mercy to such a ruffian as this, and if any harm befalls us the fault will rest entirely with yourself."

"I am quite willing to bear the blame," replied the vicar calmly. "In fact, at present we do not know but Richard may be mistaken. I am by no means satisfied that it was a man he saw in the garden."

"It wasn't a shadow, at any rate," exclaimed Richard Martin, a little nettled at the doubt that had been thrown upon his testimony. "Besides, I saw it move away as plainly as ever I saw anything in the whole course of my life."

"Probably," suggested his master, "that was only the effect of an over-excited imagination."

"But I saw enough of the fellow to swear to him at any time."

"Indeed! Pray what sort of man was it?"

"A very ferocious-looking one," replied Richard. "His figure was tall and gaunt, his complexion dark; and as for his eyes, they seemed to strike fire all the time he was listening at the window."

"'Tis he!" cried Julia, almost sinking with terror.

"Who do you mean, child?" demanded Miss Isabel, startled by her words.

"The poor girl is terrified, and knows not what she says," interrupted Mr. Dawson, unwilling that any farther explanation should take place at that moment.

"Nay," cried his sister, "you would deceive me; I am sure there is something more in all this than you choose to admit."

"Julia is still thinking of the strange man we met in our walk," said the vicar. "I told you before that she was a good deal alarmed, and now I suppose she thinks it must be the same person who has followed us home."

"And don't you think it very likely she is right in her conjecture?"

"It is possible, certainly," replied her brother; and then, afraid lest any further questions should be asked respecting their meeting with the stranger, he prevailed upon the two ladies to go to bed, promising to keep watch till daylight should give assurance that danger was at an end.

Mr. Dawson would have dispensed with the services of Richard Martin for that night, but the faithful fellow insisted upon keeping him company, and shortly afterwards he made his appearance, armed with the aforesaid blunderbuss and kitchen poker, which latter article he sagely remarked would be of great service when all the ammunition was gone. His caution, however, proved unnecessary, for during the night nothing occurred to cause them the least alarm.

See page 34.

CHAPTER IX.

THE NARRATIVE.

MANY days passed, and as nothing more was either seen or heard of the stranger, even Miss Isabel Dawson herself began to think that Richard must have been mistaken when he fancied some one was in the garden watching them. The poor fellow himself, however, was as positive as he had been at first, and long after others had ceased to think any more of his marvellous story, he continued to keep his nightly watch, lest, as he said, the enemy might steal upon them when they were unprepared.

Julia, in her own mind, felt certain that the story was right enough, though she would not admit it to Miss Isabel, who she was anxious to lull into a state of security. Each passing day, however, made her more desirous to hear the promised narrative of her benefactor, and several times she was going to remind him of it, but that she thought he might have his own reasons for postponing it till a future opportunity. At length, when she was one morning sitting at work, Mr. Dawson requested her to follow him into his study, and after a few preliminary observations, he commenced his narrative in the following words,—

I have told you, my dear Julia, that I am the son of a plain English farmer, who had little to bestow upon me except the blessing of a liberal education. At some inconvenience to himself he sent me to a superior school, and then finding that my inclination was to enter the church, he taxed all his means to complete my studies at the University of Oxford. There I passed through my different examinations with credit to myself, but as nothing is to be hoped for without patronage, I struck into another path, and through the recommendation of a friend, was received as tutor in the house of a person of fortune, whose son was to receive his education at home. Whilst there, I became acquainted with a young and beautiful female, between whom and myself ensued a friendship that ripened into the most pure and devoted love. She was an orphan, who had been placed under the guardianship of an artful lawyer, but having discovered that he was trying to obtain possession of her fortune, she took the resolution of leaving his house, and sought protection in the family where I afterwards went as tutor.

I have said that I loved her, Julia, but the meanness of my own circumstances, and the lowly situation which I then filled, prevented an explanation which I felt it would be criminal to make, when the difference in our worldly situation was considered. It seemed like presumption for one like me to aspire to the hand of Ellen Rosedale, and conscious of my own unworthiness, I forbore to give even the slightest hint of the passion that was consuming me. To be near her was a happiness greater than I ever felt before, and it was the dread of being dismissed from her presence that restrained me, when my emotions at times became almost too powerful for control. Yet there was one gratification that seemed to make ample amends for the sufferings I endured in other ways. I saw that she regarded me with favour, and in the certain knowledge that I possessed her regard, I looked forward to the future with that hope which a lover only can experience.

She was usually of a cheerful disposition, but one day on suddenly entering the room where she was sitting, I found her in tears. She was alone, and I ventured to ask her confidence, suggesting that if she was in need of friendly counsel, it might perhaps be in my power to give it.

"Alas!" she cried, "I am unworthy the friendship you have thus generously offered me. I am ungrateful, and deserve to endure the sufferings that now oppress my heart."

"Nay," I replied, "ungrateful I am sure you can never be ; so, prithee, dry up your tears, and let me see if something cannot be done to assuage this immoderate grief."

"When you know all," she exclaimed, "even you, kind as you have ever been, will join in the universal cry against me."

"Never."

"So you think now," she replied, "but when all has been revealed, you will unite with those who urge me to take a step that must render me miserable for life."

Convinced as I was that nothing would ever induce me to take part against one so beauteous, yet so unhappy, I protested that in me, at least, she should find a friend, faithful till death. She did not appear to heed me, and having wiped away her tears, she rose from her seat and abruptly left the room. At that moment I believed she was offended with me, but my melancholy reflections were broken in upon by the entrance of a servant to announce that dinner was waiting, and on taking my seat at table, I was surprised at seeing a stranger on the opposite side, who was introduced to me as Sir Edward Lindley. The meal passed amidst a silence so unusual, that I could not help observing it, and somehow or other I could not but connect the arrival of this stranger with the unhappiness that I had just witnessed in Ellen Rosedale. Each moment I grew more restless and uneasy, and glad would I have been had an opportunity offered for speaking a few words to her. At length the ladies left the room, and after taking a glass or two of wine, I was about to follow them, when Sir Edward, nodding for me to remain, inquired of Mr. Rosedale if I was aware of the motive that had led to his present visit.

"He is not," was the short reply.

"In that case," said Sir Edward, "I must request you to remain, Mr. Dawson, while I state, in the presence of our friend, that I have this day avowed myself the lover of Miss Rosedale."

He paused, as I suppose, expecting to hear my congratulation upon so auspicious a circumstance; but a choking sensation prevented my uttering a word, and I sat before him pale and speechless. Strange to say, he did not appear to observe my deep emotion, and after having paused for a minute or two, he added, with all the gaiety of an accepted lover,—

"During the period that Ellen resided under the guardianship of the old scoundrel who sought to rob her, I had the happiness of forming an acquaintance with her. Since then, however, she has much improved in beauty, and I shall esteem myself a most unhappy man in the possession of one whom all the world joins in admiring."

"Did Miss Rosedale accept your addresses?" I faintly stammered out.

"Why, to tell you the truth," he replied, "I scarcely ventured to pop the question to her, for, like most young men, I was rather gay, and believed it would be time enough to think of marriage after I had seen a little more of life."

"Perhaps, then," I observed, "your offer would not have been accepted?"

"It's likely enough that she might have been a little stiff about it at that time, for no doubt she had heard from common rumour that my love was divided among at least a dozen girls, all of whom were in anxious expectation of the time when they were to become Lady Lindley. Poor things! I dare say some of them have died of a broken heart since, but that you know cannot be helped, since the laws of England allow a man no more than one wife."

Had it been anywhere else than at the table of my patron, I should have told this heartless baronet that, as a man of honour, he had no right to trifle with the feelings of those for whom he felt no real affection. However, I restrained my indignation, and after a pause the heartless libertine proceeded.

"In spite of these little flirtations, Ellen Rosedale was the goddess of my worship. I idolized her, and resolved, when all my wild oats were sown, to make her an offer of my hand and heart. In the meantime, however, she suddenly decamped from the house of her guardian and came to throw herself upon the protection of her uncle, Mr. Rosedale. Circumstances have prevented my seeing her till now; but this day I have taken the liberty of introducing myself here, and I trust, in a very brief period, I shall be able to make a conquest of her heart."

"You have honoured me with your confidence," I said, with as much composure as I could assume; "and perhaps I may now ask if you have any motive for doing so?"

"Why, to be candid, Mr. Dawson," he said, "I have a motive; in fact, your constant residence in this house must give you an opportunity to see Miss Rosedale frequently, and I thought you might be able to give me a hint if there is any other admirer of the young lady who is likely to give me any trouble."

"Miss Rosedale has never honoured me with her confidence," I replied; "and my duties in this house do not require me to be a spy upon her actions."

"My dear sir, you mistake me," exclaimed Sir Edward, observing my indignation, and perhaps ashamed of knowing that he deserved it. "I merely thought such things might come under your observation, and if there was a rival in the way I should have been glad to know it, in order that I might shape out my course accordingly."

"I can only say," I replied, "that in all our conversations, I have never, by any chance, heard her mention the name of Sir Edward Lindley."

"Humph!" he ejaculated, "young ladies are sometimes apt to suppress the names of those they love best ; perhaps that may be the case in the present instance."

"Perhaps so," I replied, drily.

"Pray how is it, Mr. Dawson," interposed my patron, "that you seem to feel this matter so accutely—surely you don't love the girl ?"

"I respect all belonging to your family," I replied, with some confusion. "Miss Rosedale has ever treated me with affability and kindness, and in common gratitude I can do no less than return her my respectful admiration."

"That's all very well," exclaimed Sir Edward ; "but this gratitude and admiration will sometimes change into love when young people are much together. Not that I dislike a little bit of rivalry—it gives spirit to the affair, and the honour is all the greater when you carry off the prize."

"You may believe me, sir," I said, "when I declare that I have never spoken to Miss Rosedale upon the subject. Her virtue I can respect, and her beauty is such that few persons can look upon her without admiration."

"Very prettily said, upon my word !" exclaimed Sir Edward, affectedly. "All must admit the surpassing beauty of Miss Ellen Rosedale, but I think you must agree with me, that her rank and station in life place her above the reach of a mere tutor."

"Mere tutor, as I am !" I exclaimed, indignantly, "my situation is not so low but I may look for respect, even from those who conceive themselves my superiors."

"My dear sir," he said, endeavouring to gloss over his insulting words, "there is really no occasion for you and I to fall out about trifles. I was merely asking you a few questions ; and I now say again, do you think me an elegible match for the young lady ?"

"That," I replied, "depends upon whether she can regard you with affection."

"Perhaps you can pop in a word or two for me," said Sir Edward. "I will make you the mediator between us ; and if you succeed in obtaining her for me, you shall be well rewarded. I have several livings in my presentation, and, egad, you shall have the first good one that becomes vacant."

"I will owe my advancement in a sacred profession to no unworthy means," I replied, firmly. "Miss Rosedale is her own mistress, and she will be guided in the choice of a husband by her own free and unbiassed will."

"You are rather strait-laced in your notions, I see," returned Sir Edward ; "but I hope you do not imagine that I am not worthy of the hand of Miss Ellen Rosedale. For my own part, I have no doubt we should be perfectly happy together ; and the only thing that made me consult you in the affair was, an idea that it might be in your power to afford me some little assistance. Be my friend, then, and I will be one to you in return. Tell her my happiness is at her disposal ; that fortune is no object to me ; and that I would marry her if she had not a shilling in the world. These romantic professions sometimes make a great impression upon women, and why should they not upon Ellen Rosedale ? You can say, if you like, that I shall die of a broken heart if she refuses to become my wife. In short, my dear fellow, I leave it entirely to yourself to make the best you can of it. I know she will listen to anything you say, and your compliance will oblige your friend, Mr. Rosedale, as much as it does myself."

Too indignant to reply, I rose from the table, and bowing coldly to the baronet, left the room to seek the solitude of my own chamber. There, calmly and deliberately, I reviewed all that had passed, and then set myself seriously to consider what course I ought to pursue in such a case. Putting all selfish notions out of my head, I determined to weigh everything carefully before I came to a determination upon a subject of such vital importance. From the silence that had been maintained by Mr. Rosedale, I could fairly judge that he was in no way opposed to the pretensions of his guest ; and I might, indeed, take it for granted that he rather favoured the pretensions of the man who I now found arrayed against me as a rival. That Sir Edward was rich I had no doubt, and in the event of his becoming more steady and sedate, there was a probability that Ellen might be as happy with him as with anybody else. At all events it was my duty to counsel her for her own advantage ;

and sacrificing all my own hopes, I resolved to see her upon the subject, and give Sir Edward Lindley the benefit of any influence my advice might have over her. It was a bitter trial to me, my dear Julia, but honour beckoned me on, and I resolved to perform my task firmly. Having formed this resolution, I went to the window, and soon afterwards saw Ellen walking in the garden by herself. This, then, was the very opportunity I ought to take, and arming myself with all the determination, I hastened down and joined her in her pensive walk.

"When I saw you this morning," I said, "you were in tears, though what had occasioned them you would not inform me. Since then Sir Edward Lindley has thought proper to make me his confidant, and has even urged me to plead with you in his behalf."

"And have you promised to do so?" she asked, reproachfully.

"How could I refuse?" I asked. "Your guardian even seemed to wish it, and though unwillingly I have now sought an interview with you upon the subject."

"'Tis, then, as I predicted!" she exclaimed. "I told you this morning that you —even you, Mr. Dawson, would join against me."

"Surely," I cried, "you do not rank me amongst those who would persuade you to take a step that might lead to unhappiness?"

"I do not think you would do so wilfully," she replied; "yet were I to give my hand without my heart, what else but misery is to be expected?"

"You do not love Sir Edward Lindley, then?" I exclaimed.

"I do not," replied Ellen; "nor have I ever given the least encouragement to make this offer."

"You will at least pardon me," I exclaimed, "for having interfered where, perhaps, I ought to have remained silent. The task was undertaken most unwillingly, and now bitterly do I regret that, from a mistaken sense of honour, I have been induced to take a step that I see occasions you so much pain."

"You have indeed committed an error when you took it upon yourself to plead the cause of Sir Edward Lindley," answered Miss Rosedale. "We were acquainted a few years ago, when I was too thoughtless to heed the idle reports that were circulated against him. He mistook common civility for encouragement; and now, after so long a time has passed away, he must needs renew an acquaintance that I rejoiced had dropped. He professes that he would marry me without a shilling, but I know him to be deep and designing, and in spite of the cloak with which he would conceal his real views, I can see that he has motives for seeking this match that he would be ashamed to acknowledge."

"Am I to understand, then," I asked, "that your determination to reject him is fixed?"

"So much so," replied Ellen, "that no persuasion shall ever induce me to alter it. My resolution is taken—in truth, my affections are already engaged beyond recall."

"May I presume so far," I inquired, "as to ask who has had the happiness to obtain so great a treasure?"

"One," she replied, "who is not aware of the feeling with which I regard him. Here, however, I must pause—the secret lives only in my own heart, and never shall it be revealed. You have now heard a confession that has never been made to any one else; and I ask if you have not been precipitate in thus becoming the advocate of Sir Edward Lindley?"

She left me as these words were uttered, and as I revolved in my mind all that had passed, the most torturing reflections passed through my brain. Could it be me that she loved, I thought; and the more I considered her words, the more thoroughly did I feel convinced that I had lost a treasure for the want of seeking it. Almost maddened with the reflection, I hurried back to my chamber and vainly endeavoured to appease my perturbed spirits.

After a vain effort to obtain a promise of favour from Ellen, Sir Edward Lindley took his leave. I was present at their parting interview, and beheld the fury with which disappointment had filled his soul. She, however, maintained a calm dignity, and, by the resolution expressed in her deportment, he could plainly see that all hope of obtaining her hand had for ever vanished. Soon afterwards Ellen quitted the house of her uncle, and the blank which followed was perhaps the most cheerless of my life.

Within a few months from that period my pupil was sent to college, and I was endeavouring to obtain a fresh engagement, when a letter arrived informing me that I had been presented to a living some few miles off. I was puzzled to find out who my unknown friend could be, and had at length given the subject up in despair, when, by a mere accident, I discovered that it had been bestowed upon me through the intercession of Ellen Rosedale. This intelligence excited other feelings besides gratitude; it proved to me that she still remembered her former friend, and from that period I was not without hopes that we might yet be happy in each other's society.

Two years, however, did I remain without hearing anything of her, and at the expiration of that time I became acquainted with Mr. Oakley, who possesses many excellent qualities, though his temper has been soured by circumstances which it is not necessary at this moment to relate. Our friendship increased as we came to know each other better, and, at length, when the living I now hold became vacant he presented it to me, on condition that if ever I married and had a son, the boy was to be brought up to the church, and succeed me as soon as he was fit to undertake the sacred duties connected with so weighty a charge.

Having taken possession of my vicarage, and arranged everything to my satisfaction, my next care was to seek out Ellen Rosedale, and make an offer to her of my hand and heart. I found her the same kind, affectionate girl that she had been when we were formerly acquainted, and instead of appearing to be taken by surprise at my offer, she candidly confessed that her love had been bestowed upon me even before the visit of Sir Edward Lindley, and that she had resolved never to marry unless an offer was made by the man upon whom she had bestowed her affections.

In a few weeks from that period she became mine, and I may fairly challenge the world to produce two happier persons than we were. Frank was the fruit of our union; but, alas! death entered our dwelling, and my beloved wife was snatched from me at a period when—short-sighted as we all are—I was looking forward to years of uninterrupted happiness. My joy was brief, but the impression left upon my mind is never to be effaced, and from that period I have indulged in melancholy reflections that render me unwilling to seek the change and enjoyments of society. You are already acquainted with the circumstances connected with the shipwreck that caused you to become an inmate of our house, and therefore I shall now conclude a narrative that I fear has wearied you with its melancholy tenour.

"I have felt deeply interested with your recital," answered Julia. "The constancy of poor Ellen Rosedale is worthy of all praise; and deeply do I regret that you should have been deprived of her so soon after your marriage."

"It is still a source of deep affliction to me," answered Mr. Dawson; "but I bow meekly to the will of Providence, and since my boy has been spared I can still see enough to be truly grateful for."

"Ah!" cried Julia, "let us hope there is yet abundance of happiness in store for you."

"Truly, my love, I have no right to complain," answered the vicar. "You, among other blessings, seem to have been sent to console and comfort me in my old age. Your joyous spirits passed away many a weary hour, when I should otherwise have been a prey to my own mournful reflections; and, as I watched the growing excellencies of your mind and disposition, I could not but acknowledge that the tempest which drove you on our shore had conferred upon me a blessing greater than I could ever have anticipated."

"Yet it would hardly be fair," said Julia, with forced cheerfulness, "that I, an interloper in your family, should deprive Frank of any portion of his father's love."

"My heart can love both of you," replied Mr. Dawson; "and Frank, I am sure, possesses too noble a soul to grudge any portion of the esteem I bestow upon you. I love him dearly, Julia; but for all that I have never yet confided to him the story I have just related. His spirits are too light and buoyant to commiserate with the distress I have endured, and for that reason I have forborne to tell him that which he would perhaps scarcely care to listen to."

"Your sister," observed Julia, "is of course aware of all you have been telling me?"

"She is," replied the vicar; "and I need hardly tell you that her grief was nearly as great as my own when Ellen was so unexpectedly snatched from us. From that time she has had the entire management of my household affairs, and never shall I forget the tenderness and affection with which she welcomed the Ocean Child when first she was placed under her protection."

"And that tenderness has never ceased," cried Julia, anxious to bear testimony in favour of her kind protectress. "I must have been a sad plague to her, and yet she seems to regard me with as much affection as if I had been her own child."

"To do her justice," replied Mr. Dawson, "I believe she would think no trouble too much as long as she believes that anything she does is adding to my happiness. At times she is rather apt to be a little bit self-willed, but where there are so many excellent qualities to counterbalance it, we can easily overlook a little infirmity of temper. To be sure I was rather angry with her at one time, for taking such special pains to spoil Frank with excessive indulgence, yet now that he is too old for that, I can see her partiality for him without fear."

"She does indeed love him," exclaimed Julia, "and though she does not say much about it, I can observe the deep anxiety with which she is expecting his return home."

"And that will be in a very short time," said Mr. Dawson.

"I thought," said our heroine, endeavouring to conceal her anxiety, "something was said the other day about his having been offered the situation of tutor in a family of title."

"Such an offer has been made," replied the vicar; "but I believe, if he accepts it at all, it will not be just yet. In the letter I received from him the other day, he expresses a great wish to spend some little time among us, and he also sends a message to you, expressing his joyful anticipations of happiness at again meeting with his former playmate and companion. He has been devoting all his spare time to the study of music, so that I suppose we shall have nothing else when he makes his appearance here."

"It is very kind of him," said Julia, "for I really believe he never cared anything about music till I expressed a wish one day that he could play the flute so as to be able to accompany me when I play the harp or piano. From time he commenced studying it, and really, when he was at home last, he made very excellent progress in it."

"Yet had anybody else suggested such a thing to him," observed Mr. Dawson, smiling archly, "I very much question whether he would have paid any heed to it. But it is a great thing, my dear Julia, to be a favourite, and that I am sure you are with Frank, who never thinks anything too great a trouble when it is to oblige his little companion."

"I have nothing to complain of on that score," replied our heroine, who did not exactly understand the meaning of her kind friend. "He has ever been a brother to me, and my most earnest prayer is, that he may never cease to feel the same fond regard for me."

"Amen! with all my heart," exclaimed Mr. Dawson, fervently, and before the conversation could be resumed, Richard Martin tapped at the door to say that dinner was on the table. Upon this announcement Mr. Dawson and Julia proceeded to the dining-room, where they found Miss Isabel sorely puzzled to conceive what they could have to talk about all the morning.

CHAPTER X.

THE LOVER.

A WEEK after the conversation between Mr. Dawson and our heroine, a chaise was seen driving up to the door of the vicarage, and scarcely had the steps been let down than out leaped Frank, who, without waiting for ceremony, rushed into the house to greet those who he knew were anxiously looking for his return home. Nor was Richard Martin forgotten by the young collegian, and so hearty was the salutation with which he was received, that the old man winced and jumped about the room with the pain which had been inflicted by the merciless grasp of his young master.

But it is impossible to describe the joy with which Frank Dawson greeted our youthful heroine; he folded her in his arms, kissed her blushing cheek with the familiarity of an old acquaintance, and over and over again expressed the unbounded joy he felt at thus once more beholding her. Julia felt half-ashamed at being saluted by her former playmate, who had now grown into manhood; but she saw that the vicar looked on approvingly, and even Aunt Isabel, though rather formal in her notions of propriety, gave no indication, by word or look, that anything was wrong in the manner of the young people's meeting.

At length Frank proposed a walk in the garden, and, while arm in arm, they were strolling up and down, they talked of old times, and then who so happy as they? Frank could recollect a hundred diverting stories, and Julia could laugh at them as she had at the time, and so happy did they now feel in each other's society, that neither of them had the least inclination to go into the house till they had had their little gossip of old times fairly out.

"You don't recollect when I first saw you, though I do," said Frank, in allusion to their happy days of infancy. "You were then a baby lying on my dear old aunt's knee, and child as I then was, I thought of you just as I do now — that you were the prettiest girl I ever saw."

"You have not forgotten your old habit of flattery, I hear," exclaimed the laughing girl.

"How can truth be called flattery?" he demanded.

"The one is sometimes so hard to distinguish from the other," returned Julia, "that very little reliance can be placed on it."

"Well, we will not fall out for a little difference of opinion," said Frank, "so now, to change the subject, tell me, dear Julia, if I have ever been thought or cared for during my long absence?"

"Both," she replied, without hesitation; "how, indeed, could it have been otherwise with one who has ever regarded you as her brother."

"Brother!" exclaimed Frank, with evident chagrin; "is that all, Julia?"

"How else could I think of you?" she demanded. "Have we not been brought up as brother and sister from our earliest infancy?"

"Ay, ay, that's all very true," replied Frank Dawson; "but then you must remember that we are no longer children, and our regard changes its complexion with advancing years. Of course, by this time, you have heard that we are in no way related?"

"Your father has told me the story of my first appearance here," answered our heroine, "and sad enough it made me when I could no longer regard myself as his child. I thought of you, too, and how awkward we should feel when we next met each other as strangers."

"Not as strangers, at any rate, dear Julia," exclaimed the young man. "We have always loved each other, and surely this discovery need not make us look upon each other with coldness."

"Not exactly with coldness," she replied; "but it must not be forgotten that our conduct towards each other will now be regarded with watchful eyes."

"Only by my father and my good aunt Isabel," answered the young man, "and we have both experienced their indulgence so often that we surely have but little to apprehend from any censure from either of them. Nay, so far from it, that I am certain nothing will ever afford them so much pleasure as to see us conduct ourselves towards each other as we have always been used to do."

"That is, as brother and sister," exclaimed Julia, still seeming not to understand him.

"Brothers and sisters sometimes fall out," replied Frank, "and that, I hope, will never be the case between you and me."

See page 42.

"Heaven forbid!" cried our heroine, earnestly.

"You do not seem so free and unconstrained as when we last saw each other," exclaimed Frank, in a tone of gentle reproof. "I am no longer loved as I used to be, and bitterly do I see reason to regret that my father has revealed a secret that has brought about this woeful change."

"My benefactor did it from the kindest and most honourable motives," answered Julia. "He avoided trusting me with the secret till he could do so no longer, and when he saw the grief with which his narration filled my heart, he bade me still regard myself as his child, and added an assurance that I might still rely upon the same parental affection that he had ever bestowed upon me."

" That I am sure of," said Frank ; " but what, pray, said my Aunt Isabel, when she saw that my father's discovery had made you unhappy ?"

" She was more vexed than ever I remember to have seen her before," answered Julia. " She was even angry with your father for a whole day afterwards, declaring that he had better by half have held his tongue, since the explanation could do no good, and might make me unhappy for the rest of my life."

" I thought that was the light she would see it in," exclaimed the young man ; " and, to tell you the truth, I am pretty much of her opinion. You were happy enough whilst ignorant of the heavy affliction that had occurred during your infancy, and I can see no reason why you should have been told of the shipwreck till something transpired which might afford a reasonable hope that a discovery of your relations was about to take place."

" 'Tis, perhaps, better as it is," said Julia, after a pause ; " for if I had not heard the story from your father I might have been told some garbled statement that would have made me still more unhappy. Now, however, I know the truth, and never can I manifest sufficient gratitude for the humanity and kindness that rescued the Ocean Child from a fate, at the bare thought of which her soul recoils."

During the time they had been thus engaged in conversation, Mr. Dawson and his sister had been watching from the window as the young folks, almost unconscious of all else, were walking up and down the garden. Miss Isabel's eyes glistened with delight as she thus stood gazing upon them, and with a rapturous exclamation, she said,—

" Ah ! my dear brother, how happy does yonder sight make me. The idea that Frank would one day seek our young favourite for his wife, has long occupied my every thought ; and now, it seems, my most anxious and pleasing hope is about to be realized."

" You are more sanguine in this matter than I am," replied her brother. " The young folks love each other doubtless, because they have been brought up so much together ; but it must not be forgotten that there are weighty reasons why Julia should not become the wife of my son."

" What do I hear ?" cried Miss Isabel with indignant surprise ; " weighty reasons why the young people yonder should not become man and wife ! Why, surely you must be crazed !"

" Not so much crazed as you imagine," answered Mr. Dawson, calmly. " I speak not without previous thought, and again I say, I fear the union you desire can never take place."

" And why may it not ?"

" Because I would not afterwards have it said that I encouraged and brought about an alliance between my son and one whose station in life is far, very far, above his own."

" Indeed ! And who knows but her station may be inferior to his own ?" demanded Miss Isabel, rather more sharply than was her wont.

" We have no one's evidence, certainly," replied her brother ; " but we have a right to infer that she belongs to a wealthy, if not to a noble family. The clothes in which the child was found were such as would have been obtained only by those who have riches at their command."

" That's all very true," said the lady ; " but, on the other hand, we have to recollect that the poor girl would have perished but for us. You have brought her up as your own child, given her an education fit for a princess—and, in fact, done all that a parent could have done for a favourite child."

" And when all this has been said," exclaimed Mr. Dawson, " you can only claim for me the merit of having done my duty."

" But it is not every one that does his duty," returned Miss Isabel ; " and as you have done yours, I think you ought to be rewarded for it."

" I am rewarded !" exclaimed the vicar—" amply rewarded in seeing that I have conferred happiness upon one, who, but for me, might at this time be pining in poverty and despair."

"And yet you would break the hearts of those young people by preventing their union?"

"Really, my dear sister, you are too premature in your conclusions!" exclaimed Mr. Dawson. "You are speaking of their marriage, and yet neither you nor I know whether such a thought has ever entered into their minds."

"Look at them as they stroll up and down, yonder," said Miss Isabel, pointing in the direction of the young folks; "look at them, I say, and then doubt if you can that they love one another!"

"As brother and sister, perhaps," returned the vicar, smiling at her earnestness.

"Nay, 'tis nothing of that sort," she replied. "I can see they are over head and ears in love; and if you don't choose to hold out a little encouragement to them, I shall take it upon me to do it myself."

"Then you will act without due consideration," answered her brother, seriously; "and by such a course may occasion more unhappiness than you will ever be able to cure. I have thought as anxiously upon this subject as yourself, and though I cannot promise to encourage their passion as I would wish, I shall never throw any obstacle in their way."

"Come!" exclaimed the old lady, "that's speaking a little more reasonably, at any rate; and if we go on in this way, there is a chance of our understanding each other a little by-and-bye. For my own part, I cannot but regard it as a special act of Providence that Julia was thrown in our way as she was; and if ever—as poets say—marriages were made in heaven, I am sure this was."

"In that case," replied her brother, "of course nothing can occur to prevent it, so you may make yourself perfectly safe upon that point."

"I do," replied Miss Isabel; "our dear Frank's anxiety to visit home, instead of accepting the situation that was offered him, proves how he feels upon the subject; and as for Julia, though I have never been able to draw from her a word about it, I think I know her heart too well to believe that she will give pain to one whom she so long regarded as a brother."

Here Mr. Dawson suffered the conversation to drop, and in spite of all Miss Isabel's endeavours, on various subsequent occasions, to get him again upon the subject, he resolutely declined saying anything till he knew for certain whether there were any real grounds for believing that Frank sought the hand of our heroine.

Months passed away, and though the young man still remained an inmate of his father's house, nothing was hinted about his views, and it might therefore fairly be imagined that Julia, for some reason of her own, had forbidden him to mention it at present. Meanwhile, however, they continued on the same intimate terms, and Miss Isabel, who began to grow impatient at so unaccountable a delay, still entertained sanguine hopes that the day was not far distant when her anxious wish would be realized.

Six months had elapsed since Frank's return home, and during that time Mr. Oakley had been a frequent visitor at the house. The old gentleman seemed to take a pleasure in the attachment that he observed between the young people; but his perceptions were tolerably quick, and the more he saw of them the more he became convinced that the love felt by Julia for Frank Dawson was rather that of a sister for a brother than the deep, hallowed affection that inspires the heart of a woman for the object of her choice. He, however, thought all this would be made right enough in time, and, mindful of the arrangement he had made years ago with the elder Mr. Dawson, he determined that Frank, who was now in orders, should take possession of the vicarage without delay. The subject was soon afterwards mentioned, and on the day when the arrangements were to be completed, Mr. Dawson and his family were invited to dine at the mansion of their excellent patron. Never did Mr. Oakley appear to him in higher spirits than on the present occasion, and on the cloth being removed, he circulated the bottle with a rapidity that threatened to have rather a serious effect upon the heads of his guests. At length, finding that Mr. Dawson and his son declined to fill their glasses so often, he produced a huge pocket book, and taking from it three bank notes of a hundred pounds each, placed them in the hands of Frank.

"That, my dear boy," he exclaimed, "is a present that I have always promised myself the pleasure of making you by way of a start. The vicarage is now yours whenever your father can conveniently resign it, and I will take care to make him a recompense fully equal to the loss he sustains. This money will do to commence housekeeping with, and if my little favourite, Julia, will but condescend to super-intend your domestic affairs, I shall have lived long enough to see all my anxious hopes realized. Nay," he continued, addressing our heroine, "do not blush so, my dear, at a suggestion that, if followed, will, I am certain, ensure the happiness of more than one person here. Frank loves you, and I am much mistaken if you do not return his passion, so, when next you have a *tete-a-tete* together, remove his doubts at once, and frankly acknowledge that you are willing to be his bride."

Julia scarcely heard half that was uttered by the plain-speaking old gentleman, for her confusion was so great, that she buried her face in her hands, and gave way to a flood of tears. She could make no reply when Mr. Oakley brought his strange harangue to a conclusion, and Miss Isabel Dawson, observing the distress of her young friend, rose from the table, and led her to another room. It was in vain, however, that she sought to compose the agitation of her favourite, and, as Frank almost immediately afterwards joined them, the old lady thought her absence would be most desirable at such a moment, and she accordingly left the room, in order, as she said to herself, that the lovers might be under no restraint.

"My dear Julia," exclaimed Frank, when they were thus left alone, "the abrupt speech of Mr. Oakley has filled you with confusion and dismay. My father, however, has since remonstrated with him about it, and he now sends me to make his best apologies for having spoken so plainly in the presence of other persons."

"Tell him, then, he is already forgiven," cried Julia; "nay, I know not but I owe him some apology in return for having left the room as I did."

"How could you do otherwise," asked Frank, "after so extraordinary a display of the old gentleman's rhetoric? And yet, dear Julia, he has only put a question to you that I have not hitherto had courage to ask myself. Say then, since we are upon the subject, if I may hope at no distant day to make you mine?"

"Do not, I implore you, press me for an answer now," cried Julia, timidly. "When children, we loved each other as brother and sister; but now, in the un-certainty that envelopes my family, I feel that it would be wrong to encourage your addresses."

"Why need the mystery you speak of interfere with our happiness?" asked her lover. "My father knows, and I have every reason to believe, approves of our regard, and it only requires your assent to make me the happiest of men."

"Indeed, Frank," she cried, "you must not think me unkind or ungrateful, but I have anticipated this moment with a feeling of dread that I cannot describe. I felt but too conscious that I possessed your love, and my heart told me that I was unworthy of it."

"Unworthy of it, my love—Julia!" exclaimed the young man, with surprise. "What am I to understand from your words? Is it possible that your regard can have been bestowed upon another?"

"I love none other," answered our heroine; "yet do I feel that for both our sakes, it would be better that nothing more should be said upon this subject till it has been maturely weighed."

"You do not know, then," he exclaimed, "that you can entrust your happiness to my keeping?"

"Believe me, there is no one else that I love as I do you," answered Julia. "I only ask for delay in order that it may be seen whether a discovery of my friends is likely to take place, so that you may judge whether she you love is worthy to become your wife."

"Can there be any doubt of it?" demanded Frank. "Have we not known each other from childhood, and is this the time to ask if you are worthy to become the sharer of my heart and home? Rather let the question be reversed, and inquire if

I am worthy to possess a treasure that even a monarch might envy. Besides, the discovery you speak of may never occur, and would you thus cruelly delay my hopes when my happiness is so entirely at your own disposal?"

"Let your father decide between us," cried Julia; "his judgment will be our safest guide, and whatever opinion he may give, I will solemnly promise to abide by it."

"Why," asked her lover, "should we consult him, when I so well know that he will not throw an impediment in the way of our happiness? He has ever loved you as his child, and the greatest joy of his old age will be to see you the wife of his son. Say, then, that you will be mine, and I shall be happy."

"On one condition," she replied, after a pause, "I will give the promise you ask for."

"Oh, name it," he exclaimed; "and most joyfully will I accede to your terms."

"It is, then," answered Julia, "that you will not urge me to give you my hand till I am of age."

"I do agree to it," returned Frank, rapturously. "But say, dearest, why do you then seek to postpone an event that I look forward to with so much anxiety and hope?"

"Merely," she replied, "because I think, in that interval, I may hear something to resolve the mystery that involves me. Should it prove that I am the child of humble parents, it shall still be in your power to release yourself from any obligation; but should it, on the other hand, appear that my birth is equal or superior to your own, I shall proudly bestow myself on one whom I know too worthy of all my regard."

"Thanks, a thousand thanks for this noble instance of your generosity!" cried Frank, throwing himself at her feet. "Your words, dearest Julia, have raised me to the highest pinnacle of happiness, and most willingly do I assent to the postponement of our marriage till the time you have mentioned. From henceforth I will look forward with joyful hope to the moment that is to bestow upon me so fair a reward."

They were now interrupted by the entrance of Miss Isabel, whose eyes glistened with delight as she saw Frank at the feet of her they both loved. She, however, forbore to make any remark about the circumstance, but informed them that her brother was anxious to return home at an early hour, and begging to know if they were ready to accompany him. To Julia this interruption was a considerable relief, and following her friend from the room, she left Frank to meditate upon the bright scene that had just dawned upon him. In less than half an hour afterwards they bade farewell to their hospitable host, and the carriage drove off towards the vicarage. But though Frank tried to introduce a conversation, the journey homewards proved as silent and uninteresting as need to be.

CHAPTER XI.

A NEW NEIGHBOUR.

About a fortnight after the declaration of Frank Dawson, a messenger arrived at the vicarage from Mr. Oakley, to announce that the squire would not be able to spend the day with them as had been agreed upon, in consequence of his having been attacked with an alarming fit of illness. Upon further inquiry it was ascertained that he considered himself to be in danger, and besides sending for an attorney to arrange his worldly affairs, he had requested that Julia and Frank would call and see him with as little delay as possible, as he had an anxious desire to see them ere he took his leave of the world for ever.

A request like this could not, of course, be refused, and a couple of horses having been ordered to be got in readiness, the young folks mounted and took the nearest road that led to the house of Mr. Oakley. But it was in vain that Frank tried to talk his companion into good spirits; she was that day more than usually dull; perhaps in consequence of the bad news she had heard of the squire, but let the cause be what it might, she replied only in short sentences, and then relapsed into her former pensive train of thoughts. The lover thought this rather strange, but he was not easily to be thwarted, and so he kept on his rattling way, sometimes pointing out to her notice a beautiful prospect, and at others endeavouring to turn the conversation on the subject of their approaching marriage. But still he could not succeed in prevailing on her to converse freely, and in this way they had proceeded about half their journey, when Julia uttered a loud scream, and directing her eyes towards a thicket, seemed as if looking for some object that had alarmed her.

" For Heaven's sake, my dear Julia, what is the matter?" exclaimed Frank, startled from a reverie into which he had just fallen. " Tell me, I entreat you, why do you look thus terrified and direct your eyes towards yonder spot?"

" Did you not see a man pass across the road, and enter that thicket?" she demanded, in trembling accents.

" I saw no one," he replied, endeavouring to soothe her trepidation; " and even if I had, the circumstance would not have alarmed me, since, in a public road like this, it cannot create much surprise to see people passing to and fro."

" Ah!" replied Julia, " but he whom I saw has no good purpose in thus throwing himself in our way."

" You know him, then?"

" I have seen him before," she replied, " and from the moment of our interview have always had the greatest dread of ever meeting him again."

" Is he a foe?"

" That I cannot answer for; but, most certainly, he is no friend."

" A rival, perhaps."

" For an answer to that question," returned Julia, " I must refer you to your father."

" Has he, then, seen the man that just now alarmed you so much?"

" He has."

" What excuse does he offer for throwing himself in your way?"

" He professes to have it in his power," answered Julia, " to unveil the mystery that has so long obscured my birth."

" Why does he not do it, then?" asked Frank. " The service would be great, and he is certain of receiving a handsome reward for his pains."

" The reward he demands," answered our heroine, " is such as I am sure you would never agree to. The only terms upon which he will consent to reveal all he knows are that I shall become his bride, and leave the country with him immediately afterwards."

" The villain!" exclaimed Frank; " has he the presumption to make such a proposition?"

" It was made to my benefactor."

" And what said my father to it?"

" He remonstrated with him," replied Julia, " and when it became evident that the man was resolute in his demands, a direct negative was given him."

" Would to Heaven I had been there instead of my father!" exclaimed Frank

" 'Tis well you were not," replied our heroine, " for your warm temperament could never have endured the violent audacity of the man I am speaking of. Nay, the ruffian drew his knife, and your father would surely have been sacrificed on the spot had not Richard and a few of his friends arrived, and compelled the would-be assassin to effect his escape."

" How is it," asked the young man, " that I have never heard of this before?"

" Because I was in hopes we should never hear or see anything more of him," replied Julia; " and I thought it unnecessary to excite your alarm unless he should again be seen in the neighbourhood."

" It seems he is here, then," exclaimed Frank, " and if he remains much longer it's likely he and I may happen to cross each other. In fact, there is nothing I should like better, for if we do come in contact I will give him something to remember me as long as he lives."

These words were scarcely uttered than the report of a pistol was heard, and a bullet whistled close by Frank's head. Hastily desiring Julia not to stir from the spot where she was, he rode to the place from whence the weapon seemed to have been discharged, and leaping from his horse, he rushed, heedless of all consequences, into the thicket. It was in vain, however, that he looked about for the cowardly ruffian; no one was to be seen about the place, and after a fruitless search of about half an hour, he remounted his horse, and hastened back to Julia, who he found trembling with apprehension lest any fatal accident should have befallen him.

"Have you seen the ruffian?" she eagerly demanded.

"No," he replied; "the rascal knew better than to abide the vengeance I had in store for him. Thwarted in his murderous design, he took to his heels and sought safety in flight. But he shall not escape me so easily, for by and by I will have a search after him, and the scoundrel shall yet meet the punishment he deserves."

Apprehending a second attempt upon their lives, they now rode onwards at a more rapid rate, agreeing between themselves that nothing should be said about what had occurred, since it would only give rise to alarm, and thus defeat the ends of justice by giving the ruffian an intimation that flight alone could save him. At length they reached the house, and the sorrowful faces they there encountered, told them but too plainly that they had arrived too late. The old gentleman had been suddenly taken with a fit, and expired before medical assistance could be procured.

The attorney who informed them of these particulars, then acquainted them with the fact that he had been sent for by Mr. Oakley to add a codicil to his will, the effect of which was to leave a couple of thousand pounds to Frank Dawson, and a similar sum to Julia on the day that she gave her hand to his young friend. There were a few minor bequests intended as tokens of remembrance, besides an annuity to Mr. Dawson, which was to commence from the day on which he resigned the vicarage to his son.

Oppressed with melancholy thoughts, Julia and her lover prepared to return home, taking care however, to choose another route in case the ruffian should be lying in ambush to make another attempt on their lives as they returned. In consequence of this precaution no interruption was offered them, and they reached the vicarage where the melancholy result of their visit was announced, to the unfeigned grief of Mr. Dawson and his sister.

At the end of a week the funeral obsequies were performed in the presence of nearly all the tenantry, every one of whom regretted the deceased as a kind friend, who was ever ready to relieve distress, and to assist those whom misfortune had crushed beneath its deadening weight. The old squire being thus laid in the grave, they next began to wonder what sort of a landlord they should find in his successor, but on this point they were not kept long in suspense, for a few days afterwards Lord Mayfield arrived at the mansion, and as his first act of authority was to discharge all the old domestics, and replace them with creatures of his own, the impression made in the neighbourhood was anything but a favourable one.

Each succeeding day served to multiply the reports that circulated to the discredit of Lord Mayfield, though from the same sources of information it was stated that his son and heir promised to prove all that their most anxious wishes could desire. But it was to the father that they had to look at present, and from the testimony of all who knew anything of it, it appeared that he was addicted to almost every vice that the most abandoned can be guilty of. His whole life had been one continued course of dissipation. He was a gambler, a spendthrift, and a libertine, and the few persons who associated with him, were, as may be imagined, equally worthless with himself. The wife, whom he had married when a young man, bore a most exemplary character for virtue, but his harsh treatment had compelled her to quit his house, and she was now living in retirement, whilst her reprobate husband was squandering his fortune upon the very lowest outcasts of society.

Such was the character of Mr. Oakley's successor, and it may well be imagined that few who esteemed the old squire, felt inclined to form an acquaintance with the libertine lord. He seemed, however, particularly anxious to ingratiate himself with the family of Mr. Dawson, for he had heard of Julia's surpassing beauty from Jasper Hemmingsly who had formerly been one of his companions ; and thinking it easy to make a conquest in that quarter, he determined to lose no time in obtaining an introduction at the vicarage. In accordance with this plan, therefore, he called upon Mr. Dawson, and assuming his most plausible manner, declared how happy he should be to form an acquaintance with a man of whom he had heard so exalted a character. The vicar, however, perfectly well understood what all this meant, but as he wished to avoid being on bad terms with so near a neighbour, he expressed his gratification at being honoured by a visit from his lordship. Being thus far successful, the visitor invited the family to dine with him on that day week, and then took his departure, perfectly well satisfied in his own mind that he had made an excellent beginning for the designs he meditated against Julia.

But Mr. Dawson was not to be thus easily imposed upon by the fulsome compliments that had been paid him, and rightly judging the real intentions of his lordly neighbour, he went on the day appointed, accompanied by Frank, but leaving the two females at home, as being a far more appropriate place for them. When Lord Mayfield saw that he was baffled, he could scarcely restrain his anger; but as a manisfestation of his displeasure would only serve to betray him, he merely expressed his sorrow at being deprived of the ladies' society, and welcomed the father and son with as much warmth as he could, under the circumstances, assume.

Numerous other guests—the worthless satellites of his lordship—were invited to meet the party; and long before dinner was over the vicar and his son began to repent that they had accepted the invitation, since those they were thrown among gave such evident proof of their worthlessness. When the wine began to circulate, the conversation grew even more licentious; and at length, wearied with that which was so abhorrent to their nature, they made an excuse to leave early, and quitted the house with a determination never again to enter it while in the occupation of its present possessor. Their departure afforded no small gratification to those upon whom their presence had been some restraint, and all joined in expressing their satisfaction that the two gentlemen had taken their departure so early.

From a few words that had passed in the course of conversation, Frank Dawson could plainly understand that a plan was already in progress to snatch Julia from him, and the next day he sought an opportunity to see her alone, and by warning her of the design that was formed, to prevail on her to name an earlier day for their marriage than she had mentioned on a former occasion. When first he spoke of the danger she was threatened with, Julia listened to him with alarm ; but at length, thinking it impossible that such baseness could exist in any human breast, she said,—

" Really, my dear Frank, I begin to believe you are alarmed for me without cause. Lord Mayfield, I admit, does not bear the most amiable of characters, but a certain person, whom I will not mention, is said to be painted blacker than he is, and I therefore cannot think quite so badly of our new neighbour till further proof is shown."

" Nay, my father will bear witness with me that the society he keeps is disgraceful !" exclaimed Frank. " Their conversation proves them to be reckless villains ; and, as Lord Mayfield approved of all that passed, there is every reason to believe that he is as worthless as the rest of them."

" Still," she replied, " that does not argue that he has formed any design against me."

" To me it does," answered Frank ; " and, upon consideration, I have reason to believe that the scoundrel who shot at us a short time ago, is a confederate of his."

" Jasper Hemmingsly a confederate of Lord Mayfield !" cried the astonished Julia.

" I have no doubt of it," replied her lover ; " and if something is not done to thwart the treachery, I am afraid both you and I shall have to repent when too late."

" And pray how do you propose to thwart it ?" demanded our heroine.

" By our immediate marriage," he replied.

"Nay," she exclaimed, "you remember the agreement we made the last time we spoke together on this subject."

"I do," murmured Frank. "You promised to give me your hand when you were of age, and rejoiced did I feel at even so distant a prospect of happiness."

The arguments urged by Frank for an earlier marriage at length induced Julia to consent that, if she could gain her aunt's consent, she would become his wife at the expiration of twelve months.

See page 66.

Mr. Dawson now approached to ask his son to take a walk with him, and, glad of the opportunity that offered itself, Julia left the room, and hastened to the apartment of Miss Isabel, who had lately shown symptoms of decay that threatened a termination of her life at no very distant period. To her Julia revealed that portion of the conversation which related to the subject of their marriage being fixed for an earlier period than had been previously intended. The old lady seemed to be much gratified at this intelligence, but shaking her head mournfully, she foretold that ere that time arrived, she would be carried to her grave.

And her prognostication proved to be but too true, for her constitution gradually sunk under the accumulation of diseases with which she was attacked, and each week that passed away served to show but the more clearly that she was fast hastening to that bourne from whence no traveller returns. Neither kindness nor medicine could avail to sustain sinking nature, and after a few months' suffering, she expired in the arms of Julia—her last prayer being for the happiness of those whose union she had so much desired to witness.

CHAPTER XII.

SUSPECTED DANGER.

THE deep affliction occasioned by the death of Miss Isabel Dawson had the effect of postponing the projected marriage of the young people till after the usual period of mourning had expired.

But at length, when the news was spread abroad that Lord Mayfield was expected to return shortly into the neighbourhood, Frank began to grow seriously alarmed for the safety of Julia, and to consider within his own mind how the danger might best be avoided. It is true, when he reflected calmly upon the affair, there were chances in his favour that he thought not of before. The libertine nobleman, wild and reckless as he was, could scarcely venture to show the cloven foot in a place where it was his interest to gain all the respect he could, and, even should there not be that restraint upon him, Julia was so well loved and respected throughout the neighbourhood, that any plot devised against her would bring down upon the perpetrator a storm of indignation and revenge that would not be easily quelled. But at length, other things, that wore a threatening aspect, came to his knowledge, and then, wound up to a state of the greatest alarm, he sought an interview with her for the purpose of urging an earlier day for their marriage.

" Do you think, then, our marriage would check the danger you apprehend?" asked Julia.

" I should at least have a husband's right to protect you," replied Frank ; "and though my profession teaches peace, I feel that in such a cause my power would be equal to my determination to preserve you from the snares of a villain."

" Indeed, Frank," cried our heroine, " I am half inclined to think your anxiety in my behalf is without any real foundation."

" My fears," returned Frank, " are not so groundless as you imagine, for within the last three hours I have heard something that convinces me danger is much nearer than either you or I have suspected."

" Still," exclaimed Julia, " you do not tell me what it is I have to fear, and thus am I left to endure all the tortures of uncertainty. Tell me, dear Frank, how you discovered any plot formed by this reckless nobleman for my destruction?"

" He works in secresy and darkness," answered the young man ; " yet, from a report that has just reached me, I have but too much reason to believe that he has emissaries to assist him when all is ripe for the execution of his purpose. The truth is, that finding persuasion is in vain, he will now try the effect of force. They tell me the ruffian, Jaspar Hemmingsley, has been seen lurking about the place for some days past, and, if the report is true, we may easily guess who has employed him, and for what purpose he has again made his appearance in this neighbourhood."

" But is it certain," she asked, " that the person who has been seen lurking hereabouts is Jaspar Hemmingsley?"

" It's the rascal that frightened you and master at the abbey ruins," said Richard Martin, who had entered the room while Julia was speaking, and whose freedom of speech was always pardoned in consideration of his long and faithful services.

" When did you see this ruffian last?" demanded Frank, eagerly.

" About ten minutes ago, in the lane yonder, just where the four roads meet together. As soon as ever he saw me coming he bounded over the hedge, and was gone nobody knows where. I returned home as fast as I could to let you know what had happened, that young master might do as he thinks proper about sending people to look after him."

" The search will prove a vain one, I am afraid," exclaimed Frank ; " yet something must be done, since there can be no doubt that the fellow's designs are of a mischievous tendency. At all events it shall be my task to render his visit here as uncomfortable as possible. Scouts shall be watching for him in every direction, and if he is not careful we shall have him yet in safe custody."

" But, indeed, Frank, you do not look to the consequences," exclaimed our heroine. " We know him to be revengeful, and should he imagine that you are taking an active part against him, we cannot tell to what dreadful extremity his rage might carry him. Even your life, I fear, would no longer be safe from the fury of this implacable enemy."

" What mean these fearful words, my dear Julia ?" asked Mr. Dawson, who just then approached them. " Surely you do not anticipate so fearful a deed as that which forms the subject of your conversation."

" The truth is, father," replied Frank, " she is somewhat alarmed by the re-appearance of a man who, I believe, you have seen on a former occasion. In short, Jaspar Hemmingsley is prowling about, and I have my suspicion that he is employed by Lord Mayfield for some villanous undertaking."

" Against whom ?"

" Julia, as I imagine," replied the young man ; " but, of course, it is a mere matter of conjecture, and therefore all we can do at present is to watch the actions of the enemy carefully, and thus be prepared to thwart their villanous projects."

" May I ask what plan you have proposed ?" asked Mr. Dawson.

" I have suggested that our marriage should take place sooner than was originally proposed," answered the other. " Julia's chief motive for asking for delay is to consult you upon the subject ; may I inquire if you would counsel a postponement of our union, when it is certain that her own safety is involved ?"

" Your question," replied Mr. Dawson, " involves some little difficulty, and I would, therefore, rather decline giving an answer till the affair has been submitted to me by Julia herself. How say you, my dear girl,—am I to be the arbitrator between you and Frank ?"

" Most certainly," she replied ; " you are my only guide when difficulties arise in my path, and your counsel shall ever be the rule of my life."

" It is my desire that whatever judgment I give may not be misunderstood," returned Mr. Dawson. " When once an agreement has been made, it should be held sacred by both parties, unless good reason should be produced to reverse it. Julia has told us why she still adheres to her former resolution, and none can doubt the purity of her motives ; but, on the other hand, it seems she has an enemy watching for her destruction, and the next question that arises is—ought she not to take prompt measures for insuring her own safety ?"

" Very wisely argued," exclaimed Frank.

" At any rate," answered our heroine, " it seems to be so far in your favour."

" And in your own also, I hope," said Mr. Dawson, " or I would not have given the opinion. It seems, however, that you have been unfortunate enough to attract the attention of our aristocratic neighbour, whose character bears too many blemishes for anybody to doubt the motives that actuate him. Of honour I believe he has not a particle, and, if all that is told of him be true, nothing but the protection of a husband can shield you from his baseness."

" Then may not his vengeance fall heavily upon Frank, when he finds to whom he owes the disappointment of his schemes ?" demanded our heroine.

" Why," replied Mr. Dawson, " cowardice and villany so often go together, that we may consider ourselves tolerably safe from his lordship's violence."

" From his violence, I grant you," replied Julia ; " but may he not in secresy pour all his vengeance upon your son ?"

" If he could do it without fear of punishment in return," answered Mr. Dawson, " there is no saying to what extent his depravity might lead him. He however, knows that our suspicions would be immediately fixed upon him, and so far we may consider ourselves safe. His evil practices are directed against helpless women, but I never yet heard that he had courage enough to venture upon exciting the wrath of a more powerful adversary."

" I have no fear of the consequences of his disappointment," said Frank. " If Julia will consent that our union shall take place within a few weeks, I think all will be well."

Thus urged, Julia was obliged to consent, and that day month was fixed for the celebration of a ceremony which was to ensure her future happiness.

CHAPTER XIII.

CHANGES OF FORTUNE.

Alas! for the instability of human affairs. The whole of the residents at the vicarage were looking forward with joyful anticipation to the day fixed for the marriage of Julia with Frank Dawson, little thinking of the storm that was gathering in the horizon. Preparations in a simple yet extensive style were made, for it was expected that rather a numerous party would honour the vicarage on that day, the worthy clergyman being much respected in the neighbourhood. But a week of the allotted time had to elapse, when one morning, Frank, who had been out for a ride, was absent for some hours. Several servants were sent out in search of him, and when they returned, it was with the body of the unfortunate young man, who to all appearance had been thrown from his horse, and killed on the spot. But there were some who whispered that Jaspar Hemmingsley knew more of Frank's death than would have been safe for him to have owned to.

However this may have been, he immediately disappeared from the neighbourhood, and though the strictest search was made for him, no trace of him was ever afterwards discovered.

Who can picture the despair of the doating father—who describe the grief of the young bride? The vicarage was indeed a house of mourning, and our poor heroine found all her powers of consolation called into requisition to soften the grief of the bereaved father.

Weeks passed away, and Julia saw with the greatest alarm that Mr. Dawson was rapidly sinking beneath the effects of the last affliction, and ere the winter had passed away, she stood by his bed of death.

Oh! what anguish was it for poor Julia thus suddenly, and on the very verge of happiness, to be left a friendless and lone being to the mercy of an unpitying world! Death, with a reckless hand, had snatched away all who loved her, and she was now unprotected, and exposed to all the dangers which beset the path of a young and beautiful woman.

Mr. Dawson, her kind benefactor, Isabel, Frank, Mr. Oakley, were all gone, and that, too, within so short a time; and now she was left to act for herself, with as little experience of the world as she could well have.

Julia, immediately she could summon sufficient composure, had written to Mr. Philip Dawson, the brother of her benefactor, requesting him, as heir-at-law, to hasten to take the direction of affairs at the vicarage, but her letter received no answer.

With a heavy and aching heart, she compelled herself, with the assistance of Richard Martin and Susan, to superintend the arrangements for the funeral, and then she saw the father laid by the side of his son.

The day of the funeral was a melancholy one to Julia, and when she returned to the vicarage, she shut herself in her chamber, and gave vent to her grief in tears.

On the morning of the next day Julia was informed that a gentleman wished to see her, and when she entered the drawing-room, she found there a fashionably dressed man, who announced himself as a Mr. Loosely, commissioned from Lord Mayfield to inform her that having made a presentation of the living, the new incumbent would wish to take possession of the parsonage-house as soon as she, Miss Dawson, could make it convenient.

Julia, though she thought this haste on the part of Lord Mayfield rather premature, did not venture a remark upon it, but assured Mr. Loosely that the possession of the house should be given up as soon as the person who owned the property within it had arrived to make his own arrangements.

CHAPTER XIV.

FURTHER CHANGES.

Two days after the funeral, Mr. Philip Dawson, the heir-at-law of her benefactor, arrived, accompanied by his lawyer. The former took possession of whatever property he found belonging to his brother, and then made himself completely at home at the vicarage, where, for several days, he kept up a regular carousal, being almost constantly intoxicated.

On one of these occasions his companion, warmed by wine, offered an insult to the unprotected Julia. She fled into the garden, whither he pursued her ; and he was proceeding to offer further violence, when he was felled to the ground by a violent blow.

Julia turned to thank her protector, who was a young man of very pleasing address, and who insisted on accompanying her to the house, and seeing her in safety. He refused to give his name, saying that he had particular reasons at that moment for concealing it ; but when she told him that she should leave the parsonage for ever on the morrow, he appeared much agitated, and implored her to let him know whither she intended to proceed. This, to a stranger, she did not feel justified in disclosing, and the stranger left her in a sorrowful mood.

The morrow came, and Julia found that the brother of her benefactor and his rascally adviser had both quitted the vicarage at an early hour, ashamed of their conduct. or, perhaps, if the truth was known, unwilling to risk the consequences that might ensue.

Immediately after breakfast she stepped into a carriage which was in waiting, and, accompanied by Susan, they proceeded to a farmhouse at some distance from the vicarage, where she had secured a lodging with a farmer of the name of Edwards, to whose family she had behaved with great kindness during the lifetime of her benefactor.

While here, at the suggestion of Susan, Julia caused several advertisements to be inserted in the newspapers, detailing the facts of her early history ; and, to her great delight, after three days of the most anxious suspense, she received a letter, containing a full description of the clothes Julia had worn at the time of the wreck, with an account of the ship and the time of its sailing.

There could be no doubt but that at length she had discovered a parent, for it was evident, from the wording of the latter, that her father was dead ; and Julia looked forward with the most delightful anticipations to the hour in which she should be clasped to the breast of her mother. The letter stated, that her mother would instantly set out to fetch her from the seclusion in which she was living, for the purpose of introducing her to the proper and more elevated sphere of society to which, by her birth, she was entitled.

At length a carriage rolled up to the farmhouse, and a middle-aged woman alighted. In the next moment Julia had fallen upon her mother's neck and was shedding tears of joy. The lady, whose name was Churchill, returned her caresses with the greatest delight, and Julia spent one of the most delightful hours she had ever experienced.

Mrs. Churchill expressed her sorrow that she should be obliged to take her at once from her humble friends, but her presence was so necessary in London that she should be unable to remain more than a few hours. Julia lost no time in packing up the necessaries she intended to take with her, and then, rewarding farmer Edwards for his kindness towards her, and bidding adieu to Susan, who declined accompanying her, as she had lately been betrothed to a young farmer in the neighbourhood, she stepped into the carriage with Mrs. Churchill, and they drove off at a rapid pace.

In the course of conversation, Julia learned that her mother was slightly acquainted with Lord Mayfield, but when she told her of the attempt that nobleman had made upon her liberty, her indignation was not so great as might have been expected. Indeed, Julia was much surprised at the coolness with which Mrs. Churchill treated the affair, and she felt inclined to attribute it to the different light which her mother's station in life might induce her to view it in.

It was quite dark when they arrived in London, and the carriage soon stopped at the door of a large mansion. On entering the house, Julia was struck with the splendour that prevailed everywhere, and was quite dazzled with its magnificence.

As Julia felt fatigued with her journey, she bade her mother good night, and was conducted to her chamber, where, from the joint effects of fatigue and the emotion she had experienced, she soon fell fast asleep.

In the morning Mrs. Churchill introduced her to her cousins—two handsome, but rather bold girls, whose manners Julia thought were rather coarse for the circles in which, by their conversation, she understood they moved.

After dinner, Julia enjoyed a *tete-a-tete* with her mother, in which she learned that her father, Admiral Churchill, had died in an engagement many years since, leaving her, Julia, a considerable fortune, but which, in consequence of her supposed loss at sea, had for years been enjoyed by the next nearest relative of the admiral ; and this relative, she added, was now inclined to dispute the identity of Julia, which would have to be substantiated by undisputed proofs.

This conversation was interrupted by the return of Fanny and Charlotte, the nieces of Mrs. Churchill, who were accompanied by two gentlemen, who they introduced as Captain Belmont and Sir Everard Calthorpe, whose addresses they were supposed to be receiving. This was another source of surprise to Julia, for both had the appearance of having spent their youth in dissipation and riot, and were considerably advanced in years.

Fanny at once declared that it was their intention to visit the theatre that evening, and pressed her cousin to accompany them. Julia at first objected, but on being rallied on her rusticity and love of solitude, she was at length induced to consent, and at the appointed time the carriage conveyed them to the theatre.

It was the first time Julia had ever visited a similar place, and she became so wrapt in what was passing on the stage as not to notice anything passing around her. As the curtain fell upon the first act, she raised her eyes for the first time, and glanced round the house. A flush of colour suddenly suffused her cheeks, for seated in a box almost immediately opposite, was the young stranger who had come so opportunely to her assistance, when she had been so grossly insulted by Mr. Philip Dawson's legal adviser at the vicarage. His eyes were fixed upon her countenance with a mournful expression of pity, and, as he caught her glance, he rose from his seat and left the box, as if for the express purpose of joining her.

A minute or two of great suspense passed, and then Julia heard the door of the box open behind her, and some one entered, and took a seat, as if determined to remain. She slightly turned her head, and to her great alarm beheld Lord Mayfield, who, with the greatest nonchalance, leaning slightly forward, said,—

"I am rejoiced at once more seeing Miss Dawson, as it gives me an opportunity to apologize to her for my conduct on the last occasion when we met."

Julia indignantly repelled his advances ; but Mrs. Churchill, hearing the name of Mayfield, turned hastily, and, in a tone of voice, the severity of which astonished Julia, commanded her to receive the apology of his lordship, who expressed himself extremely sorry that he should have ever offended.

Nothing could equal the surprise of Julia at this circumstance ; but as that was no place for explanation, she listened in silence to all that his lordship said, and waited with impatience till the play should conclude.

On the close of the first piece the party left the box, while Lord Mayfield went in search of Mrs. Churchill's carriage. As they left the saloon, the stranger again passed them, and once more he fixed upon her a mournful look, and passed slowly on. Before she could acknowledge the stranger's presence, even by a glance, Lord Mayfield handed her into the carriage.

When they reached home Julia found, to her great surprise, that a number of gentlemen were carousing in the lower apartments, and their mirth had assumed a character little in accordance with Julia's ideas of propriety. She therefore at once retired to her chamber, and sought her bed.

CHAPTER XIV.

MORE SUSPICIONS.

WEEKS passed away, and, to Julia's surprise and disgust, Lord Mayfield became a constant visitor at the mansion, and Mrs. Churchill never let an opportunity pass of urgently speaking in his favour. Julia was the more surprised at this, as she knew that her mother was fully aware that his lordship was a married man, and that his character as a libertine was fully established. She avoided that nobleman, however, as much as she possibly could, but she could not help observing with pain that this behaviour gave great displeasure to Mrs. Churchill.

A visit was one evening proposed to Vauxhall, and with great difficulty Julia was induced to make one of the party, Lord Mayfield accompanying them. While there, two gentlemen passing, one of them made an observation upon the beauty of our heroine, which Lord Mayfield rose to resent. One of the gentlemen turned his head as his lordship reached them, and again Julia beheld the features of the stranger who had evidently taken such an interest in her welfare.

Lord Mayfield returned to the party considerably agitated, and whispered something to Mrs. Churchill, who immediately rose to leave. Julia made an inquiry as to who the stranger was, but Lord Mayfield returned an evasive answer, though she learned sufficient to assure her he held as high a position in society as his lordship himself.

Julia had hardly reached her room to retire for the night, when one of the servants knocked at the door, and requested to speak a few words with her.

Julia complied with her request, and from her she learned, to her great horror, the truth of the fears she had all along entertained. The servant had had a quarrel with Mrs. Churchill, and now, in a spirit of revenge, came to disclose to Julia a plot which had been laid for her destruction. Lord Mayfield had seen the advertisement, and caused Mrs. Churchill, a woman of infamous character, to answer it, and to personate Julia's mother; and this woman's sole efforts, for the time Julia had been with her, had been directed to her ruin. The nieces, added the servant, were as bad as Mrs. Churchill herself, and the gentlemen, Captain Belmont and Sir Everard Calthorpe, had them at that time in keeping.

For some time Julia sat absorbed in the terrifying reflections caused by her situation; but, at length, aroused by her fears, she resolved to leave the house, taking with her the few valuables she possessed. In a few minutes after forming this resolution, she stood in the open street.

For some time Julia wandered in the streets, unknowing whither to turn her steps, until, overcome with fatigue and excitement, she sank, fainting, before some railings. Here she was found by two working men, who, thinking she was intoxicated, raised her up, for the purpose of conveying her to a place of safety. At this moment a gentleman came up, and he paused to see what was the matter. At that moment Julia opened her eyes, and what was her astonishment to recognise, in the individual who was bending over her, the stranger whom she had seen under so many circumstances.

The gentleman also instantly recognised her, and appeared to be much shocked at her situation; but a few words from Julia were sufficient to give him an idea of the true state of affairs, and, placing a purse of gold in her hand, he confided her to the care of one of the men, who offered to procure her a lodging with his mother, and then left them, saying he would return in about a quarter of an hour.

The instant the stranger left, Julia, who feared nothing so much as being again thrown into the power of Mrs. Churchill, prevailed upon the men to conduct her to the nearest coach-office, and when the stranger returned to the spot, the whole party had vanished.

The stranger who had shown such an interest in the fate of Julia, it may now be necessary to state, was no other than Lord Ashbourne, the son of Lord Mayfield, who had been on a visit to his father's mansion, where he had first seen Julia, and was struck with her beauty and innocence. He had heard of her departure with her new-found mother, and when he had again beheld her in London, it was in company with Mrs. Churchill, who, he learned, was of a more than suspicious character.

Lord Ashbourne had kept a strict watch upon the house of Mrs. Churchill, and he could not help feeling regret that Julia should still continue a willing guest of a woman of such a degraded character, and he longed to make her acquainted with his suspicion. Nothing could equal his surprise on meeting her in the street, on the night of her escape, and when he returned to the spot, expecting to find her still there, his disappointment was great on finding the spot deserted.

The next morning, very early, he called at Mrs. Churchill's, fancying, perhaps, by some unlooked-for circumstance, she had again fallen into her power; but from that person, who had not then discovered the escape of our heroine, he received an evasive answer.

On reaching his home, Lord Ashbourne found the whole establishment in the greatest confusion, and, on inquiry, he learned that his father, Lord Mayfield, had just been brought in mortally wounded. He hastened to his father's room, where he found him lying almost insensible on his bed, with his mother, in tears, by his side.

His lordship had been at a gaming-house on the previous night, where he had lost a considerable sum of money, and a duel ensuing, the result of a quarrel, he had received the ball of his adversary in a mortal part. A few hours closed a life of profligacy; but, before he died, he confessed the part he had had in the abduction of Julia, and implored his son to seek her pardon.

As soon as his father's affairs could be arranged, Lord Ashbourne instituted a strict search after Julia, and on visiting the neighbourhood where she had passed her youth, he learned from Susan, who was still unmarried—the farmer, Edwards, who had proposed for her having turned out to be an impostor in the pay of Lord Mayfield, for the purpose of preventing her from wishing to accompany Julia to London—that our heroine had secured a retreat at Brighton, where she was then living.

We will now return to Julia, who, when she reached Brighton, had sought a temporary lodging at an inn kept by a woman of kind-hearted disposition, named Fuller, in whose house she had been seized with a brain fever, which confined her to her bed for several weeks. On her recovery, she found that, notwithstanding the kindness of her new friend, her little stock of money was reduced to a few shillings, and her situation was becoming truly distressing when she obtained, through the recommendation of the surgeon who attended her, a situation as companion to one Lady Ramsay, with whom she remained till unpleasant circumstances, caused by the receipt of a letter from Lord Ashbourne, now, since the death of his father, bearing the title of Lord Mayfield, again compelled her to quit.

This letter, under the impression that it was from the nobleman who had so cruelly persecuted her, and of whose death she was not aware, she had torn into a thousand pieces, and she thus remained in ignorance of its kindly contents.

On our heroine's quitting the protection of Lady Ramsay, she again sought her worthy friend Mrs. Fuller, the landlady under whose roof she had experienced that illness which had seized her on her arrival in Brighton. About a week afterwards, while walking in the streets, she, to her great joy, encountered Mr. Capel, who was equally overjoyed to see her. From him she learned that he had never received one of the many letters she had written to him, and that his business in Brighton at that moment was entirely unconnected with herself. On learning her condition, he procured for her the situation of governess in the family of a Mrs. Markham, the mother of a young man who had, but a short time since, married one of the worthy curate's daughters. In this situation she became a great favourite of Mrs. Markham's, and her great beauty attracted the attention of that lady's nephew, Sir Edward Digby, who commissioned his aunt to offer Julia his hand and fortune.

See page 58.

Julia, though her young hopes had been sadly blighted by the untimely death of Frank Dawson, cherished the memory of Lord Ashbourne, a stranger as he was to her, in her breast, and, in spite of the pleadings of both Sir Edward and his aunt, she remained firm in refusing to listen to the suit of the latter, who at last quitted Brighton, resolving to hide the pain Julia's determination gave him from the sight of his friends.

CHAPTER XVI.

THE DISCOVERY.

LORD ASHBOURNE had waited very impatiently for a few days for an answer to the note which he had sent to Julia while she was residing at Lady Ramsay's, and then, not receiving any, he had taken the liberty of calling at her house. The answer he obtained from that lady was far from satisfactory, and thus he found himself once more without any clue to the whereabouts of our heroine, and he returned to London in a desponding state of mind.

One day, while overlooking a cabinet belonging to his father, he discovered, to his great surprise, in a secret drawer, a miniature, the resemblance of which to Julia was so great that for a moment he could not help feeling a pang of regret steal over him that she should so far have countenanced his father's addresses. He placed the picture in a secure place, and the subject afforded him conjecture for many a weary hour.

Restless with anxiety, he determined to pay a visit to the Stanmore estate, which had come into his mother's possession on the death of her brother, the late Lord Stanmore. On visiting the mansion, he was shown over it by an old woman, and he was particularly struck by a picture of its late master, which he conceived bore a great resemblance to himself; which opinion was further confirmed by his guide, who said that a young woman living with a lady in the neighbourhood, and who, from the description she gave of her, he conceived to be Julia, had expressed great emotion on beholding the picture. On inquiry, Lord Ashbourne learned that the lady with whom the supposed Julia was living resided but a short distance from the spot, and, in her youth, had been betrothed to the original of the picture.

When the young nobleman gained this information, he leaped into his saddle, and in a very short space of time he was in the grounds of Mrs. Markham's mansion. To his great joy he beheld Julia seated reading, and, presenting himself before her, he apologized for the abruptness of his appearance.

An agitated interview ensued, in which Lord Ashbourne reproached Julia for flying from him on the night of her escape from Mrs. Churchill's, and then he detailed to her the unsuccessful search he had instituted for her—Julia learning for the first time that the letter she had received at Lady Ramsay's had been from him, and not from his father.

Drawing the miniature from his breast, the young lord, with as much delicacy as he could assume, asked Julia whether she had ever presented it to his father. The agitated girl, indignant at such a supposition, broke from Lord Ashbourne, and fled from the spot before the latter could detain her.

Her refusal to answer his question appeared to Lord Mayfield like a tacit acknowledgment that his torturing doubts were not unfounded, and, furiously dashing the picture upon the ground, he rushed with headlong speed from the place, unmindful of whither he was directing his steps.

The excitement, however, was too great for Julia, and before she had proceeded far she fell insensible to the ground, where she was found by one of the servants, who also picked up the miniature not far from the spot.

Julia was conveyed home, and a physician was sent for, who, finding that she had been seized by a violent fever, would not let her be disturbed, and it was only by the most assiduous attention that she recovered ; the cause of her sudden illness remaining an impenetrable mystery to Mrs. Markham, who, however, did not press upon her any inquiry respecting it.

Sir Edward Digby had renewed his visits to the Hall, and his attentions were received as those of a favoured brother, but not the slightest encouragement was given by Julia to the renewal of his suit. She was at length persuaded to take an airing with Sir Edward in his carriage, and, in their ride, to Julia's surprise, they encountered Captain Belmont, whom she had seen as the pretended suitor of Fanny at Mrs. Churchill's. That gentleman now rode up to the carriage, and in an insolent manner saluted Julia, expressing his satisfaction that he beheld her so well protected. Having uttered these words in a sneering tone, he galloped off, Sir Edward following him with his eyes flashing indignation till he was out of sight.

In reply to her companion's question respecting her knowledge of the captain, Julia was obliged to say that she had seen him at a house where she had been stopping for some time. This answer appeared to satisfy Sir Edward, and calling the groom, who was riding behind, he ordered him to follow the gentleman, and bring word where they were putting up.

When they returned to the mansion, Sir Edward left Julia, and sought the stable, where he found his groom, who had just returned, having watched them to an hotel in a neighbouring town. Providing himself with a brace of loaded pistols, he sought the hotel, and was there told that Captain Belmont and a friend were strolling in the neighbourhood.

Sir Edward, after a short search, discovered the pair, and at once demanded that the captain should retract the words he had spoken, or make an apology to the lady he had insulted.

Belmont refused, and persisted in asserting that he had known Miss Dawson under circumstances justifying the words he had used. Sir Edward grew indignant, and striking the captain in the face, he branded him with the name of coward, and producing the pistols he had brought with him, insisted on instant satisfaction.

Arrangements were instantly made, and after an exchange of shots, the captain was stretched on the grass, wounded, but not seriously, in the thigh.

While his friend proceeded to the town for a surgeon, Captain Belmont confessed to Sir Edward that he believed Miss Dawson had been entrapped into the hands of Mrs. Churchill at the instance of the late Lord Mayfield, and that she had suddenly made her escape before any attempt could have been made upon her virtue.

On the return of the captain's friend with the surgeon, all fears as to the result of the wound were set at rest, and after assisting his late antagonist into the carriage, and seeing it drive off, he turned away on his road to his home.

CHAPTER XVIII.

THE HISTORY OF A LIFE.

MRS. MARKHAM and Julia heard the result of the duel from Dr. Barton before any of the newsmongers of the neighbourhood had conveyed it to the mansion, multiplied by a hundred exaggerations, and Julia could not help feeling the most poignant regret that one she respected so much, and to whose dearest friend she was so deeply indebted, should have risked his life for her sake.

A conversation respecting Sir Edward Digby naturally ensued between Mrs. Markham and Julia, in which the former took the opportunity of again pressing the suit of her niece, but with no better success than before. It was during this conversation that Julia impressed Mrs. Marknam with a sense of the depth of her gratitude for the kindness of that lady, by relating the whole events of her life, from the first discovery and rescue by Mr. Dawson, up to the very moment of her interview in the gardens of the mansion with Lord Ashbourne, and its result.

"Since then," added Julia, "I have seen nothing of him, and doubtless he will carefully avoid meeting me in future."

"In that case," exclaimed Mrs. Markham, "you can have no excuse for rejecting the offer that has been made by my nephew."

"Do not urge me upon that subject just at present," cried our heroine; "for much as I regard Sir Edward Digby, I feel that it will be impossible to bestow upon him an undivided heart."

Mrs. Markham had often promised Julia that she would relate to her the circumstances of her own early life, and as the evening had not far advanced, she took that opportunity of fulfilling her promise.

In her youth, Mrs. Markham had been betrothed to the young Lord Kendall, the brother of the present Lady Mayfield, and preparations had even been made for the wedding, when the young lord showed an unaccountable repugnance to the match, for which his bride could only account by the supposition that his affections had been estranged from her. He would have deferred the union for some months, wishing to travel abroad, but the Earl of Stanmore, his father, whose mind had been set upon the projected marriage, had threatened him with his eternal displeasure, if he did not at once accede to his wishes.

At length Lord Kendall, with the greatest agony of mind, had confessed to his affianced bride, that he not only loved another, but that he was actually married, and implored her forgiveness and intercession with his father, whose anger he dreaded.

Stricken as Mrs. Markham was by the despair this communication inflicted upon her, she did intercede; but all was in vain, and Lord Kendall, who had also offended his wife's father, was obliged to quit England with his wife, to eke out a scanty living on a foreign soil.

Years passed away, and Mrs. Markham became a wife, her despair at the blight thrown over all her youthful hopes having settled down to a calm melancholy. At length the Earl of Stanmore was seized with a dangerous illness, and then she wrote a letter, supplicating him to forgive his offending son; but the only concession the dying man would make, was to instantly draw out a fresh will, leaving the whole of his property to his son's children, if he ever had any.

Upon hearing of his father's death, his lordship determined to return immediately to England. The last that was ever heard of them was that he, his wife, with an infant, and one attendant, embarked on board a vessel from one of the French ports. Unfortunately, however, the ship encountered a severe gale, and went down, within sight of the Sussex coast, and it was never ascertained whether any on board was saved."

When Mrs. Markham had concluded, Julia could not help remarking upon the similarity of the circumstances that had attended the death of the unfortunate Lord Kendall and his family, and those which had consigned her to the care of Mr. Dawson, the more especially as the dates tallied exactly.

Mrs. Markham was particularly struck with these remarks, and could not help conjecturing that Julia might indeed be the offspring of that unfortunate nobleman.

Upon further talking the matter over, and comparing various circumstances together, Mrs. Markham came to be more than ever of opinion that her young friend was indeed the daughter of the unfortunate Lord Kendall. She, however, would not say too much to excite hopes that might end in disappointment, and it was eventually agreed, that they should consult with Dr. Barton as to the course it would be best to adopt.

CHAPTER XVIII.

THE MEETING.

THE course of our narrative now compels us to return to the young Earl of Mayfield, who, it must be remembered, left our heroine, at their last interview, under circumstances that were likely to produce a lasting estrangement between them.

He returned to London, and on reaching his home, his mother, to his great surprise, showed him a letter addressed to the Earl of Mayfield, evidently from Julia, which had fallen into her hands. Its contents at once removed all doubts of her innocence from his mind, and with a heart throbbing with joy he narrated to his mother the history of his acquaintance with Julia.

The Countess of Mayfield, it will be recollected, was the sister of the unfortunate, erring Earl of Kendall, and consequently in his youth had been the friend of Mrs. Markham, and now, when her son informed her that Julia was residing with that lady, she resolved to renew that intimacy for his sake, and endeavour to forward his suit as much as possible. This determination she expressed to Lord Mayfield, and nothing could equal his joy when he heard it.

The next day a letter was despatched to Mrs. Markham by the countess, announcing her intention of paying her a visit, excusing the absence of the company of her son on the plea of ill health. This was pleasing news to Mrs. Markham, though it raised a crowd of conflicting emotions in the breast of Julia, and the arrival of the countess was looked forward to with some anxiety.

On the third day afterwards the Countess of Mayfield arrived during the temporary absence of our heroine. The meeting between her ladyship and Mrs. Markham was such as might have been expected from friends who had been separated so many years. The visitor, however, was impatient to hear all the particulars she could gather from Mrs. Markham, and breaking off a conversation that related more to family affairs, she broke forth into a eulogium of the young stranger that was founded, as she acknowledged, upon the glowing description that had been given by her son.

At these concluding words Julia, who knew not of the visitor's arrival, entered the room. Lady Mayfield advanced to meet her, but as she did so a change came over her countenance, and sinking into a chair, she exclaimed,—

"What is this I behold?—the form, the face, the image of my hapless brother's infant! Tell, tell me, Julia—whence came you, and who are your parents?"

"That," sighed our heroine, "is a mystery that years have not yet unveiled. I have ever been called the Ocean Child, because in my infancy I was saved from shipwreck."

"Merciful Heaven!" cried Lady Mayfield, "in this stranger, then, have I discovered the daughter of my hapless brother, Lord Stanmore!"

With the affection of a parent the countess clasped our heroine to her bosom, and for some few moments both of them were unable to give expression to the words of joy and thankfulness that struggled for utterance. On recovering themselves, however, the clothes which had been worn by Julia when rescued from the waves, were produced, and the sight of them confirmed the previous suspicion, for it so happened that they had been presented to her relative by Lady Mayfield, and, from a variety of circumstances, she could most positively identify them.

The countess now listened with delight to a recital of all the circumstances connected with the discovery, by Mr. Dawson, of the Ocean Child; and then, in as concise a style as she could, she put our heroine in possession of the history of her parents after they had quitted England, under the displeasure of their parents.

At length the party separated, and Julia, retiring to her room, threw herself upon her knees, and poured out her thanks to the Almighty for the happiness he had bestowed upon her.

CHAPTER XIX.

A JOURNEY PROPOSED.

At a much earlier hour than usual on the following morning, Julia rose, and throwing on her dressing-gown, proceeded to the apartment of Mrs. Markham, who woke at the moment her young friend entered the room. Surprised at so early a visit, and fearing that it portended some fresh disaster, she eagerly inquired the reason of her unexpected appearance before her.

"Do not let my presence alarm you, my dear madam," cried Julia, "for this visit has been occasioned solely by my own restlessness, and being unable to remain longer in bed, I came hither that we might speak together without fear of interruption."

"You look pale and agitated, my love," exclaimed Mrs. Markham. "Why do I see these tears, Julia? Why are you thus sad, when so much has occurred of late to render you happy?"

"Alas!" she sighed, "I fear happiness and I are doomed never to hold a long acquaintance together."

"And yet the wish I have so often heard you express, has at length been fulfilled."

"I know it is ungrateful of me to murmur," replied Julia; "but my heart is oppressed with a weight that seems too great for endurance, and even in the midst of this joyful change, there remains something that calls forth my regret."

"Have you not a title, my dear girl?"

"True."

"And a large estate to support it?"

"I have," answered Julia, "but the discovery which has just taken place, will deprive another of that which he believed to be his own."

"You mean the Earl of Mayfield," observed Mrs. Markham. "It is true he loses something by this recent affair, but the consequence need not be so serious as you imagine. He loves you, and, as I believe, not without a return of your affection. Yield therefore to his solicitation, and with your hand bestow upon him the wealth which you have thus unexpectedly acquired."

"It is evident from your words," replied our heroine, "that you have not observed Lady Mayfield with the same searching scrutiny that I have myself. Throughout our various conversations she has scarcely once mentioned the name of her son, and there can be little doubt that she favours some other alliance for him that may prove more advantageous."

"My dear Julia, you wrong her by this suspicion," exclaimed Mrs. Markham. "Besides, Lord Mayfield has expressed the love he bears you, and, judging from his well known honour, I feel certain that he will seek no other bride till he has received your positive refusal."

"Let us hope he will never put me to such a trial," answered Julia. "His mother appears to entertain no wish that such a union should take place, and when, according to promise, I relate to her the story of my own life, it shall be my chief care to omit all mention of the acquaintance that has subsisted between his lordship and myself. Of Frank Dawson only will I speak, and her ladyship shall be assured that my heart lies buried beneath the green turf that covers his grave."

"But in doing so you will prevent the offer which I believe Lord Mayfield intends to make."

"Let it be so," replied Julia, "since I can make any sacrifice rather than afford uneasiness to his mother. I have said that his name shall not pass my lips during the narrative I am about to give, and it is now my earnest request that you will not in any manner lead to it."

"Nay, your concealment of so important a fact will appear like deceit."

"Yet you will give me the credit to believe that I am above dissimulation," replied Julia. "Her ladyship shall learn that I have once loved one from whom death has separated me, but there is no necessity for explaining the tenderness with which I have regarded her son."

"But most likely," observed Mrs. Markham, "he has already mentioned it to her."

"That is but too probable," answered our heroine; "yet even in that case there is no necessity for me to mention it unless pressed by her upon the subject. So urge me no more to change my determination, for my mind is fully made up on the subject. Give me your assurance not to mention my name in connection with that of Lord Mayfield, and I shall be satisfied."

"Can you not then repose confidence in her as a relation who has your interest at heart?"

"I do indeed regard her both for her kindness and the tie of blood that unites us," answered Julia. "There is every reason to love Lady Mayfield, but you are my earlier friend, and in you only can I repose the secret thoughts of my soul."

"Really, Julia, this is the first time I have seen reason to accuse you of being romantic," returned Mrs. Markham; "however, I cannot refuse your request, and you may therefore rest assured that I shall not break the confidence you have reposed in me. But in making this promise, I must candidly confess that it is not done without repugnance."

Mrs. Markham having by this time finished her toilette, the two ladies descended to the breakfast parlour, where they found Lady Mayfield just concluding a letter to her son, in which she narrated the discovery that had taken place, and the reduction which it would occasion in his income. This, however, she felt assured would afford no regret on his part, and having despatched the letter by a servant, she requested Julia to relate, as she had promised to do, the chequered history of her life. This was instantly complied with, and when at length she came to a conclusion, her ladyship expressed her surprise at one omission which our heroine seemed studiously to have made.

" You have freely opened your soul to me, my dear niece," she said ; " but not once have you mentioned my son, though I was anxious to hear in what way your acquaintance with him commenced."

" I have avoided doing so, my lady," she replied, " because it would have led to a subject which, at present, I am anxious to avoid. At present you will, therefore, be kind enough to pardon me if I remain silent upon the only point on which I have observed any secresy."

She left the room on uttering these words, and as Lady Mayfield thought it would not be fair to speak any further upon the subject during her absence the conversation was changed, till the two ladies rose from the breakfast table to prepare themselves for a stroll through the ornamental grounds that surrounded the house.

On the third day afterwards Lady Mayfield received an answer from her son, in which he expressed his own gratification at the discovery which had taken place, and even spoke with cheerfulness of the alteration it would make in his own affairs. Still, as Julia was the undoubted heiress of the Stanmore estates, it was his determination to give them up without a moment's delay, and as there were heavy arrears to pay off, he intended to sell some extensive landed property of which he was possessed, and with the proceeds to liquidate the debt which had been incurred through the supposition that there existed no other heir to Lord Stanmore than himself. The sacrifice thus made would greatly impoverish him, but he considered that honour demanded it, and when this was done he intended to travel abroad until his fortune was sufficiently retrieved to enable him to revisit his native shores under more favourable circumstances.

" What a pity it is," exclaimed Mrs. Markham, as her ladyship finished reading the letter, " that his lordship should be compelled to give up the estate, when it appears to me that it might easily be retained in his own possession."

" I understand you, my dear madam," answered Lady Mayfield ; " but there is a barrier to the union of these young folks that I fear can never be surmounted with honour. My son loves Julia most ardently, and, had she remained in her former simple state, would have married her. Such an union would have afforded me the greatest pleasure, had I seen reason to believe that it was agreeable to herself. It appears, however, that he has not gained possession of her heart, or she would not have spoken so continually of her deceased lover, without once mentioning the name of Lord Mayfield."

Mrs. Markham would have given worlds to have related all she knew upon the subject ; but the promise she had made to Julia restrained her, and after a few moments' silence she ventured to observe that, perhaps a meeting between them would serve to revive the kindly feelings with which they had once regarded each other. Lady Mayfield, however, only shook her head at this suggestion, and having remained for some little time in pensive thought, she said,—

" Should a marriage now take place between Julia and my son, it would appear to have been effected rather from selfishness than love. Lord Mayfield has ever maintained his honour untarnished, and whatever may be his feelings upon this subject, I am certain he will endure any sufferings rather than let the world believe that he seeks the marriage for his own advantage."

Had there been any excuse for breaking her promise, Mrs. Markham would at this moment have told her ladyship that Julia would never marry unless the offer came from his lordship. But her word had been passed to keep the secret inviolate, and it was with the greatest mortification that she suffered to let slip a chance by which the happiness of two young persons might have been insured. At present, however, there was no alternative, and she found herself compelled to adopt a course that might lead to much future misery.

During the period that had been occupied by the preceding conversation, Julia was seated in her own chamber, and occupied in writing a letter to Lord Mayfield. As the contents were of some importance, we shall take the liberty of looking over her shoulder, and thus be enabled to give the entire epistle in the following words:—

"My Lord Mayfield,—

"Agitated as I am by the extraordinary events that have recently taken place, I cannot at present trust myself to enter fully into the motives that have induced me to write to you. Your mother, I understand, has already explained the discovery which has taken place, and you are therefore aware of the relationship which exists between us, and without which I should not have ventured to write these few lines. Wealth and honour have fallen upon me, yet neither of them did I ever covet. During the lifetime of my first honoured benefactor, I was ever happy in the possession of all that his means could bestow. I never thought of rising beyond my station, yet fortune is now thrust upon me, and I find myself in the possession of a title and estates that cannot afford the slightest gratification to one who knows not the weakness of ambition.

"Having premised thus much, it now remains for me to urge a request which I hope your lordship will not refuse me. It would be in vain for me to conceal the fact that you are resolved to make every sacrifice, in order to pay certain arrears of rent which are due from the period of the late Lord Stanmore's death. To do this you must impoverish yourself, and think you I would ever enjoy the possession of wealth, knowing as I must the deprivations it must subject you to? In short, my lord, I was rich enough in my own estimation before this discovery took place, and since the secret which involved my birth has been explained, I have nothing more to wish for. If then you would see me truly happy, you will still retain possession of the estates, and may every happiness attend the gift which it is thus in my power to bestow. With Mrs. Markham I shall continue to reside, and as my wants are but moderate, the income left me by my benefactor will be sufficient to support me in the only station in which I can find true enjoyment. Trusting that you will make no objection to an arrangement upon which my happiness depends,

"I remain, my lord, your sincere well-wisher,
"JULIA DAWSON."

This letter having been folded and sent off to the post-office, our heroine returned to the drawing-room, where she found Lady Mayfield busily engaged in painting some rare flowers which had just been gathered for her by the gardener. She, however, rose to receive Julia with open arms, and making her sit down beside her, she once more spoke of the necessity of immediate steps being taken for possessing herself of Stanmore House, the steward of which had just arrived to take the commands of his mistress upon the subject.

"Indeed, my lady," exclaimed our heroine, "there is no need for such haste. I am not yet of age, and cannot make up my mind thus suddenly to leave a house where I have passed some of the happiest of my days."

"But I have no doubt Mrs. Markham will gladly accompany her young friend."

"That might serve in some degree to reconcile me to the change," replied Julia; "but the truth is, I have no inclination at present to launch out into the new scenes that have been opened to me."

"Well," exclaimed her ladyship, "I will not urge the subject any further just at present; but, of course, you will not refuse to accompany me to London?"

"To London!" cried Julia, with dismay; "must I, indeed, visit a place that will remind me of so many painful trials and sufferings."

"You really must force your inclination in this instance," replied Lady Mayfield, "or people will begin to give you the character of an eccentric. Besides, your visit to the metropolis will be made under circumstances very different to those which took you there on a previous occasion, and the Countess of Stanmore will meet with respect, though as Miss Julia Dawson she had little reason to be gratified with all she saw and had to endure."

See p. 60.

"If I could do so without giving offence to any kind friend," answered Julia, "I would most positively refuse to enter into scenes of gaiety for which I entertain a deep-rooted abhorrence."

"And so get laughed at for your pains, my dear child," exclaimed Lady Mayfield. "No, no, you must trust yourself to the guidance of your elders in this instance, and depend upon it I will not propose anything which can give you even a moment's pain. Besides, the London season of fashion is now at its highest, and you must be presented at court when the next drawing-room is held."

"That," cried Julia, "is a ceremony that I would avoid more than anything else."

" And why, my dear niece ?"

" Because my life has been passed in such humble obscurity that I should tremble with apprehension on finding myself among the high-born people that I should meet with in that gay assemblage of rank and wealth."

" But you are now one of them," answered Lady Mayfield ; " and I can take it upon myself to say, that there will not be one present who more deserves the world's esteem. Besides, it is a form that all persons of a certain rank are expected to comply with, and it is, in fact, necessary, unless you would bring upon yourself the sneers of the world of fashion."

" At any rate," said Julia, " I may, perhaps, be spared the ceremony during the present season. Another year I shall be more accustomed to the new station that just now sits so awkwardly upon me, and if you then recommend it, I promise to make no further objection, whatever may be my own feelings upon the subject. May I request your ladyship to grant me the time I have named ?"

" Where no control is exercised, the request is scarcely necessary," answered Lady Mayfield. " Your wish shall ever govern me, my dear Julia ; and there certainly is no need for haste, since next year will do quite as well as the present. And now, having thus far acceded, I will, in my turn, ask a favour of you."

" Oh, ask it," cried our heroine, " and I promise to yield my willing assent."

" It is, then, that you will not refuse to accompany me to London."

" I will not ; when do you propose setting off ?"

" That will entirely depend upon circumstances," replied her ladyship ; " though, to confess the truth, I care not how soon I introduce my fair niece into the society which she is fated to adorn."

" Nay, your partiality, I fear, blinds you to too many of my faults."

" Your modesty may think so," replied Lady Mayfield, " but it will not in the least alter my opinion. I am, perhaps, somewhat proud of my new-found niece ; but it is to be hoped that partiality has nothing to do with the praise I bestow upon her. However, I shall consider that a bargain has been fairly made between us ; so, as may departure for London may take place rather suddenly, I must request you to make whatever preparations may be necessary, in order that no delay my take place when the moment for starting arrives. As for dresses and jewellery, there will be no occasion to trouble yourself about them, for London is a mart where you may be quickly supplied with every necessary at an astonishing short notice. A few trunks packed up will be all that is necessary, and when once we reach London I think it will not be very difficult to convince you that your present notion of it is formed upon a very erroneous foundation."

Before Julia could reply to this, a servant entered the room to announce that a stranger had just arrived, who requested an immediate interview with the Countess of Stanmore.

" Who can it be, I wonder," exclaimed our heroine, " who has thus early discovered my change of rank ?"

" Did the person send up his name, William ?" asked Mrs. Markham, who at this period joined the party.

" No, ma'am," replied the man ; " I asked him to do so, but he said he was an old friend whom her ladyship would be very glad to see."

" Perhaps," cried Julia, with alarm, " instead of a friend, it may prove to be an enemy."

" That we will presently see," exclaimed Mrs. Markham ; " so don't make yourself uneasy, my dear child, for let him be friend or foe, there are enough of us in the house to prevent any mischief."

" Shall I desire him to walk in, ma'am ?" inquired the domestic.

" You may, William ; but remain in the next room, lest we should happen to require your assistance to remove a troublesome visitor."

The man retired, and in few minutes afterwards returned to the drawing-room, and, to the astonishment of our heroine, introduced no less a personage than Mr. Simon Briefly, the pettifogging lawyer of Philip Dawson. The visitor grinned, bowed, shrugged his shoulders, and seemed to make himself perfectly at home.

CHAPTER XX.

THE MAN OF LAW.

" YOUR ladyship is very much surprised to see me, I dare say," exclaimed the lawyer, with all the freedom of an old friend; " but the truth is, that no sooner did the news of your good fortune reach me, than I thought it my duty to neglect business and everything else to come and offer my congratulations."

" You are very kind, sir," replied Julia, coolly; " but, if I recollect, when we last parted it was under circumstances that left little room to imagine that either of us would ever wish to meet together again."

" Ah! but that's all past, and should be forgotten," exclaimed the man of law, with a low, cringing bow. " Upon my life, I couldn't believe it, when first I heard the news of your good fortune. It seemed to be impossible that times should change about so, for when my friend Mr. Philip Dawson and I came to see you last, matters were in a very queer state, and——"

" You have travelled some distance I suppose, sir?" said Mrs. Markham, anxious to put an end to a conversation that did not promise to be a very pleasant one, if she might judge from its commencement.

" Oh, I think nothing of distance when it's to serve or see a friend," replied Mr. Simon. " Her ladyship and I have seen each other before to-day, and I dare say she recollects old Phil Dawson well enough."

" I shall never forget him, sir," answered Julia, with marked emphasis; " for he gave me reason to bear him in my remembrance as long as I live."

" Ay, ay, he was a little roughish in his manners, I dare say, my lady," returned the lawyer; " it's a way he's got; though, after all, he's a worthy old soul, when you come to know him as well as I do."

" I have no wish to do so," answered Julia.

" Ah!" cried Briefly, " you still bear malice, I see. But, to come to the point, my lady, it was partly at his request that I have undertaken this long journey. You see what noble sacrifices friendship can make; though you must still bear in mind that I should have come to wish you joy of your new dignity, whether he had wished me or not. However, Phil Dawson is as honest, good-hearted a creature as ever breathed, in spite of his being now and then a little bit cantankerous, and so he sent me to pay his best respects to your ladyship. It's truth, 'pon my soul, and he was going to write a letter, only he happened to recollect that penmanship was not among his accomplishments. But where there's a will there's a way, and, as he couldn't come out in the epistolary style, he sent me with a message to be delivered by word of mouth."

" Have the kindness, sir, to be as brief as possible," cried Julia; " for you see I am already occupied with two of my friends."

" Ha, ha, ha!" laughed the man of law; " your ladyship is always in such a confounded hurry. I dare say you recollect that the last time we met you ran away from me as if I had been some terrible fellow that you were afraid of. At that time I little thought that I was trying to do the amiable with a person that was soon afterwards to be a countess in her own right. But, mercy on us! what changes have taken place since I saw the young stranger lurking about the premises, and who, after all, turns out to be neither more nor less than your own cousin. And then, dear me, how doleful he looked, to be sure, afterwards, when he couldn't find out which way you had taken on leaving the vicarage-house."

" Mr. Briefly," exclaimed the impatient Julia, " is this the only business you have with me?"

" Oh! bless you, no my lady," replied the lawyer; " but when friends meet, you know, after a long absence, it's very natural that they should talk a bit over old times."

"Then let me request," she said, "that you will leave all digression at once, and come to the business—if you have any—that brought you here."

"Well, then," exclaimed the lawyer, "my friend Phil, who is a good creature after all, though a bit of an oddity in his ways, has sent me with his best respects to your ladyship, and seeing that you have come into a title, and plenty of wealth, he hopes you won't be particular about pressing him to pay that trifling legacy his brother left you. He thinks it can't be a matter of any consequence to you now, and as he is but a very poor man, it's to be hoped you won't be so hard as to insist upon the fulfilment of his brother's will."

"And is this really the purpose of your visit to me?" demanded our heroine.

"To be sure it is," he replied.

"Then a letter, sir, would have answered all the purpose," she exclaimed, "and your long journey might have been easily spared."

"Psha! what care I for long journeys when a friend has need of my services?" exclaimed Mr. Simon Briefly. "A good nag makes everything quite easy, you know, in the shape of a journey, and so off I set as soon as ever dear old Phil told me what he wanted me to do. But that wasn't all; for, to tell you the truth, I thought your ladyship might not be engaged with a professional adviser. Of course there will be some little trouble to get the estates from the present possessor, and as I can undertake to carry on the business at a cheap rate, perhaps I may be allowed to expect the honour of your ladyship's patronage."

"Your benevolent design is frustrated," returned Julia, in accents of contempt, "for it happens most fortunately for all parties that a perfectly amicable arrangement will be made that renders unnecessary the assistance of the law."

"Well," exclaimed Briefly, "if you can't employ me just now, it's likely you may want my assistance some other day, and you will always find me ready to afford my advice whenever it may be required."

"Should I ever need your services, Mr. Briefly, I shall not fail to send you word to that effect," replied Julia. "And now, sir, you must excuse me for saying that we are particularly engaged, and must, therefore, wish you good morning."

"Ah! very good—I understand—half a word is enough for me at all times; so I shall take my leave if you will only have the kindness to say what message I am to take back to Phil Dawson."

"I have not yet made up my mind upon the subject," replied our heroine, "and, therefore, merely say that I will give it my serious attention, and in a week or two I shall send him a letter stating the determination, whatever it may happen to be."

"Very well, my lady," replied the lawyer, "I'll do as you have commanded—but, between ourselves, my ride has made me rather hungry, and a little refreshment, you know, is always acceptable to a weary traveller."

"You shall not leave without partaking of my hospitality," interposed Mrs. Markham; and as she left the room with Julia and Lady Mayfield she gave orders that Mr. Simon Briefly should be served with whatever he required.

In a very short time the lawyer was ushered into another room, where a substantial lunch was laid out for him, and to which it must be acknowledged he did ample justice. Having swallowed innumerable mouthfuls, and imbibed a fair proportion of wine, he threw himself back in his chair, and observing for the first time the butler was present, he flattered himself that it was a mark of peculiar honour paid to him. Poor Mr. Briefly! had he guessed the real cause, he would have known that it was merely a precaution taken in case he should feel inclined to put any of the silver spoons and forks into his pocket. However, vanity spared him the mortification; and glancing towards the butler, to mark the effect of his words, he said,—

"You see, my friend, with what distinction I am received here? I am an old friend of her ladyship—knew her from the time when she was a little girl—made love to her once, and might have married her, only she was poor then, and I little guessed what fortune was in store for her."

" Oh then you didn't care much about her."

" Indeed but I did, though, Mr. Steward, and should like to have made her my wife, if it hadn't been that nobody knew who she was, or where she came from. At that time she was living on the charity of a person near the sea coast, and all that I could learn of her was, that she had been found on the beach during a terrible storm, and from that circumstance she went by the name of the ' Ocean Child.' And now only think what a change has taken place in her circumstances ! The poor receiver of charity is turned into a countess, and, if report speaks truly, she is one of the richest ladies in England."

" Well," retorted the steward, " and if it is so, there's no one I know of that deserves it better."

" Very true," answered Briefly, tossing off another bumper of wine ; " she was always an excellent creature, only I hope she'll not be greedy in money matters now that a few pounds are of no consequence."

" I dare say she'll expect to have what's her own," returned the steward.

" May be you are right, my friend," exclaimed Simon ; " for some people are very particular in that respect, and look upon paltry sums as if they were of the greatest consequence. Now, the old parson that brought her up, left her a thousand or two, by way of legacy, thereby robbing a friend of mine, who was the heir-at-law. He can't afford to lose so much money, and so, to tell you the truth, I've come down here to see if I can't prevail on her ladyship to give it up to him."

Simon Briefly would not have been so communicative but for the unusual quantity of wine he had drank. Having done so, however, he suffered his tongue to run a great deal faster than his wit, and as his auditor did not care to interrupt him, he entered into a long history of the countess, the greater portion of which was pure invention.

" And so," exclaimed the steward, taking advantage of the first pause that occurred, " it seems that this Philip Dawson has the modesty to expect that my lady will give up her legacy to him, though he don't seem to have behaved over kindly to her."

" Pooh ! pooh ! can't she forget and forgive, like a Christian woman ?" demanded Briefly. " She must be talked into it, and between ourselves, I have undertaken to manage the job, and, in the event of my succeeding, I am to receive five hundred pounds for my services. But I must see her again, it seems, so perhaps you'll be kind enough to provide me with a bed in the house for a night or two ?"

" We have none here but for friends of my mistress's own inviting," answered the other ; " and as she hasn't asked you, it stands to reason that you are not wanted."

" What am I to do, then ?"

" Sleep at one of the public-houses in the village, I suppose," replied the steward. " You will find excellent accommodation there,—only I'd advise you to make haste about securing one, for when it gets late they are rather particular about taking in strangers."

" That, I suppose, is a broad hint to take myself off," observed Mr. Simon Briefly. " Dear ! dear ! that a man of my standing in society should be obliged to put up with insult from a menial. But we won't quarrel just now, most worthy steward ; so, if my horse is ready, I'll take my departure, and you may tell the Countess of Stanmore that I shall take an early opportunity to repeat my visit."

The lawyer staggered from the room under the influence of the deep potations he had taken, and clambering into the saddle with no little difficulty, he rode slowly off in case he should happen to have a fall, which he had just sense enough left to know would be highly relished by those who were watching his departure.

" Why, mercy on me, my dear Julia," cried Lady Mayfield, as soon as the lawyer was fairly gone, "who is the impertinent fellow that has come here, as if for no other purpose than to annoy and vex you?"

"He is a man that I have little reason to respect," answered our heroine; "and to tell you the truth, it was with some difficulty that I could so far control myself as to treat him with common civility."

"I have heard you speak of him," said Mrs. Markham, "as a sort of quack attorney, employed by the brother of your first benefactor."

"This is the person," answered Julia. "During our brief acquaintance I had every reason to hold him in the utmost contempt; yet he had the insolence to persecute me with an offer of marriage, though I told him from the first, that, instead of inspiring me with respect, he was the object of my contempt."

"Ay, ay," said Lady Mayfield, "the truth is, he had an eye to the legacy that was coming to you, or the proposal would never have been made. But it seems we are to be honoured with another visit, so we must now think of something that will spare us the infliction."

"As he sleeps in the village," observed Mr. Markham, "would it not be as well, Julia, if you were to write an answer to this Mr. Philip Dawson? One of the men servants can take it to the lawyer, with a message that he is to convey it with all speed to the person to whom it is addressed."

"I will do so," replied Julia, and, sitting herself down to her desk, she wrote a short note, expressing her firm determination not to yield up the legacy to one whose selfishness she despised; and, having folded and sealed the epistle, it was despatched to Mr. Simon Briefly with a message so plainly worded that he could not fail to see that any future visits could be dispensed with.

"Now," she said, as the servant left the room, "I hope there is a stop put to one of my tormentors. Mr. Philip Dawson, too, will find that I am not so easily persuaded as he imagined; and should any further application come from the same quarter, I shall take care to keep out of the messenger's way."

"The last visit," said Mrs. Markham, "is a lesson for me not to allow any strangers to see you until I have first ascertained their name and business. The caution appears to be necessary, for I dare say there will be plenty to annoy you now that the news has spread of your rise in the world."

"I trust," observed Lady Mayfield, "that our young friend will now learn that she needs the protection of a husband, however much she may feel disinclined to change her present state."

"Upon that subject, my dear aunt, I must entreat your forbearance," cried Julia. "For a time I cannot explain the motives that have induced me to prefer a life of celibacy, but it may happen, ere long, that I shall be able to afford you the requisite information, and when that is the case, I am certain you will not blame me for the course I have adopted."

"Well, then, we will say no more about it just now," answered Lady Mayfield; "though, to confess the truth, you must be prepared with a very good reason indeed to satisfy me that you have acted wisely in forming so extraordinary a determination. At no period have your circumstances been so low that you need to have laid such a restraint upon yourself, and now that a life of gaiety and pleasure is before you, it appears to be the height of weakness that you should persist in a resolution which should no longer have any control over you. However, I have promised not to say anything about it for a short period, and I will therefore remain silent on the subject till it is quite convenient for you to let me into this secret of yours."

Mrs. Markham wished most sincerely that she might be permitted to explain as much as she knew, but her promise had been given not to say anything till Julia herself assented to it, and it was, therefore, with no little mortification that she heard the half-expressed anger of Lady Mayfield at what she imagined to be a foolish prejudice on the part of her niece. Whilst she was thus perplexed how to act, a message called her from the room; her absence, however, was but brief, for ere the conversation between Julia and her ladyship could be resumed, she returned, bringing with her Sir Edward Digby, who had thus paid a visit to congratulate our heroine upon the change of fortune that had taken place in her favour since they last saw each other.

"But why," asked Mrs. Markham, "have you been so long a stranger to my house?"

"The truth is," he replied, "my heart has ever been here, but I durst not venture, unless with the certainty that my presence was welcome to Julia. When, however, I heard the changes that had taken place in her fortune, I could no longer refrain from venturing into her presence to offer those congratulations which I hope she will do me the justice to believe are sincere."

"Believe me I am most grateful," answered Julia; "more I could say, but I fear lest my words should be construed too much in your own favour."

"There is little fear of that," replied Sir Edward; "though, to tell you the truth, I could almost have found it in my mind to grow jealous of a person that I met, and who told me that he had been paying a visit to this house."

"Why, I declare," cried Mrs. Markham, "if you have not had the good fortune to stumble upon little Mr. Simon Briefly, the lawyer."

"Let him be lawyer, or physician, or anything else, I could hardly restrain my hands from giving him a sound horse-whipping," exclaimed Sir Edward.

"I wish you had, with all my heart," cried Mrs. Markham.

"It was only his utter worthlessness that saved him," replied the baronet. "He happened to be stopping at the house where I stopped to rest my horse, and with all the familiarity of an old acquaintance he began to inquire from whence I had come and whither I was going. Of course I did not satisfy him; and then, pointing to this house, which we could see from the window, he said he knew very well that I was coming here. Scarcely refraining from a hearty laugh at the fellow's impertinence, I inquired what he knew of the place or its inmates. He then told me that Julia Dawson, who was now Countess of Stanmore, was an old acquaintance of his; that he had known her when she was a poor girl, with nothing in the world to depend on but a trifling legacy that had been left by the person who had brought her up from infancy. Nay, he went so far as to boast of having been once over head and ears in love with her, and declared that he could have had her as easily as possible but for some other lover who stood in the way. Provoked at such barefaced insolence, I was about to kick the fellow out of the room, but he foresaw my design and made a hasty retreat to avoid the dishonour."

"I wonder at that too," exclaimed Mrs. Markham; "for to men of his stamp a kicking is a god-send, since it enables them to bring an action which serves to put money in their pockets. However, it is much better as it is; and since he has a notion that you are here, it is likely he will not venture to show his face among us any more."

She then led the baronet from the room, and Lady Mayfield, who had been a silent auditor of the preceding conversation, inquired of our heroine if that was not the person of whom she had heard as having a short time before proffered his addresses to her."

"It is," replied our heroine.

"And is it possible," asked her ladyship, "that you can make any objection to a man who is said to possess so many estimable qualities?"

"You know him then?"

"I have never had the pleasure of meeting him before," answered Lady Mayfield; "but report has spoken of him so favourably that I have often wished for an introduction to him. You, however, seem to have formed a less favourable opinion, though with more opportunities of discovering his virtues."

"I entertain the highest respect for him," replied Julia, "but cannot yield my hand to a man who does not possess my undivided affection."

"Come, that is a tolerable acknowledgment that your heart is given to some one else."

"I do not deny it," answered Julia.

"Yet you do not encourage the addresses even of the man you love," said Lady Mayfield.

" That," replied Julia, " is the secret that I have thus far kept from you. In truth, I know not that he regards me even with common friendship."

" In that case you are a foolish girl to bestow a thought upon him," exclaimed Lady Mayfield. " Forget him as if you had never met, and reward the constancy of Sir Edward Digby by giving him your hand."

" That I have found to be a less easy task than you imagine," replied Julia, with a sigh. " My respect for Sir Edward taught me that some sacrifice was due to his devotion, and at one time I had made up my mind to yield to his entreaties ; but the effort failed, and I have now made up my mind to live a life of celibacy rather than consent to a union with one whom I cannot love as he deserves."

" May I ask the name of the gentleman who has thus obtained possession of your heart ?"

" There are reasons why I cannot answer that question at present," replied Julia. " You are the last person from whom I ought to keep a secret, but when you know all, as sooner or later must be the case, you will acknowledge that I have not taken the course without sufficient reason."

" Well," exclaimed Lady Mayfield, " I will at least prove to you that I am not without a fair share of patience, and so I will not press you to reveal this secret till you think proper to make me your confidant. But, though I make this concession, it must be confessed that I can see no sufficient reason for the rejection of so worthy a man as this Sir Edward Digby."

" I have myself acknowledged the high regard I feel towards him," answered Julia ; " nay, he is even aware of it from my own confession, and if anything could have added to the esteem I bear this excellent man, it is the kindness with which he listened to the explanation I offered."

" Did you hold out any hope that you might hereafter be inclined to regard his addresses with more favour ?"

" I did not," replied our heroine. " Indeed I absolutely forbade him to speak to me any more upon the subject, and it was then finally arranged that we should from that time regard each other as brother and sister."

" Then you have positively made up your mind never to marry him ?"

" I will not go so far as to say that," she replied, " because in the event of the other person marrying I may consider myself as absolved from the pledge I have taken. It seemed, however, better that I should say nothing about it to Sir Edward Digby. He has now no expectation of becoming my husband, and is content to meet me in the way you have witnessed."

" But it strikes me," said Lady Mayfield, " as being very probable that he will wed some one else, and in that case you will stand a fair chance of dying an old maid."

" Nothing would afford me more pleasure than to see him the husband of some deserving woman," replied Julia. " I have even implored him to place his affections on some one else ; but hitherto he has declared that he will either wed me, or pass the remainder of his days unmarried."

" Poor fellow !" exclaimed Lady Mayfield. " I cannot help pitying him for the life of me, and if you only felt as I do, he would not have to repine much longer at his unrewarded love. However, I still hope that you will take compassion on him, for it seems tolerably clear to me that if his rival entertained any regard for you, he would have taken care to throw himself at your feet long before this time."

" Your opinion would be different if you knew all the circumstances," answered Julia. " There is indeed a reason why I have not seen him for some time past, and when you are by-and-by informed of it, you will cease to wonder at my conduct, which I am willing to admit must appear unjust to those who know not the circumstances that have produced my present determination."

The subject was now broken off by the return of Mrs. Markham and her nephew. The latter appeared to be more cheerful than he had been for some time past ; he entered freely into conversation, and by degrees grew less restrained than he had latterly been when in the presence of Julia.

CHAPTER XXI.

THE LOVERS' MEETING.

QUITTING the peaceful mansion of Mrs. Markham, we must return to Lord May-field, who, on the receipt of a letter from his mother, desired most ardently an opportunity to visit and apologise for the harshness of his conduct at their last meeting, and he would instantly have set out for the country seat of Mrs. Mark-ham, but that he felt that it would be impossible to offer a sufficient excuse to Julia for the cruel suspicions which he had so unreservedly uttered when he quitted her presence, as he supposed, for ever.

But when he received the letter of our heroine, his joy was unbounded. It is true, she therein seemed to convey an insinuation that she would never marry; but lovers are proverbially ardent in their imagination, and in the fulness of his satis-faction he believed that it would still be possible to prevail over her scruples, and thus obtain for himself a prize that he regarded as inestimable.

The noble generosity with which she had proposed to yield up to him the whole of the property to which she was the undoubted heiress, filled him with admiration. He saw at once the kindness of a heart that he had well nigh broken, and cursing his own impetuous nature, he determined to make the most humble concessions in order to convince her that all his doubts were removed. As for the generous offer she had made, he resolved on no account to accept it, unless accompanied by her hand, and having put everything in a train for the sale of such estates as might be necessary to pay off the arrears due to the young Countess of Stanmore, he set forth on his journey, feeling more like a criminal about to appear in the presence of an accuser, than as a lover hastening to throw himself at the feet of his mistress to implore her acceptance of his suit.

Two days before he commenced his journey, however, Lord Mayfield wrote a letter to his mother, explaining his former acquaintance with Julia, and the hopes he had once formed that she would have consented to become his wife. The subsequent rupture which took place between them was also slightly mentioned, and whilst he implored her to use whatever influence she might possess over Julia, he most earnestly requested that she would keep from our heroine the secret with which he had entrusted her. In the event of his failing to appease the supposed anger of Julia, he declared it to be his intention to go abroad for some few years, as he felt that it would be impossible to remain in England when so many chances might throw him in the way of one whom he had lost by his own impetuosity of temper.

Lady Mayfield read this letter with mingled emotions of sorrow and regret. She felt deeply grieved at the situation in which her son had placed himself, yet could not but own that Julia had received an insult which she was bound in honour to resent. Her sorrow was occasioned by the threatened separation from her fondly idolised Charles, and the probability, at her time of life, that she should never see him again if the project were once put into execution. There was one reason, however, why she could not consent to urge the marriage of Julia and her son. If she did, as circumstances at present stood, the world would accuse her of having done so for the dishonourable purpose of securing for Lord Mayfield the fortune to which her niece had just succeeded, and much as she desired the union, no consideration could induce her to take a step that she would afterwards have reason to be ashamed of.

Mrs. Markham observed the melancholy of her guest, but, from motives of delicacy, forbore making any inquiry into the cause of it. Believing, however, that it was occasioned by her anxiety to see Julia settled in life, she would have given the world to inform her of the tender regard which had once existed between her son and Julia. But the solemn promise that had been given to the latter restrained her from doing so just at present, and as Lady Mayfield had informed her of the expected visit of his lordship, all her hopes of the future rested on the interview that must soon take place between the estranged lovers. To be sure, she could not but see that Lord Mayfield's arrival would, in all probability, be fatal to the expectations of her nephew; but then Sir Edward Digby was not without a fair share of moral courage, when it was necessary to be called forth. He could endure misfortunes, without sinking under them, and it occurred to her that it was likely he might seek some other bride when once he discovered that all chance of obtaining the hand of Julia was at an end.

As his lordship had, in one part of his letter, mentioned the generous offer that had been made by our heroine, Lady Mayfield took the first opportunity that presented itself to speak to her upon the subject.

"I cannot," she said, "too highly praise the noble sacrifice you have made to my son; but, at the same time, I am gratified to hear from him that he has resolved, most respectfully, to decline the proposition. Indeed, my dear girl, his conduct would have been dishonourable had he acted otherwise, and never yet has an act of his come to his mother's knowledge that she need blush for."

"But I have no desire for wealth," answered Julia; "and, therefore, the sacrifice is not so great as you seem to imagine."

"At present you may think so," replied Lady Mayfield; "but I see in you the last of a noble and ancient family, which threatens to become extinct, unless you retract this hasty resolve of yours not to marry. I will not attempt to dictate upon whom you should bestow your hand, but I trust, ere long, my dear Julia will see that my anxiety is solely excited for her own advantage."

"My dear girl," cried Mrs. Markham, who had entered the room while these words were being uttered, "will you absolve me from the promise I gave? Give but your consent—say that I may repeat our conversation, and Lady Mayfield will be made happy by what I have to communicate."

"Not yet—not yet," murmured our heroine, in a paroxysm of despair.

"You are unhappy, my love?"

"I am; but will endeavour not to render others so," she said. "I know what I have to endure, and can support all without uttering a complaint. Lady Mayfield has urged me to marry; but, alas! she little knows the fatal barrier that exists to prevent my adopting her well-meant advice."

"You are resolved, then, to marry no other than the person to whom your heart is engaged?"

"Such is, indeed, my determination."

"And this is formed, though under the certain conviction that your peace of mind will be broken for ever?"

"I have often prayed for death," replied Julia; "but still I linger on in all the hopelessness of despair. Had I perished on that fatal night when my parents sank into their ocean grave, the fortune and title would have descended to him who so richly merits them. For me wealth has no charms; it oppresses me with new anxieties, and from the moment when I found myself an heiress, I have been more unhappy than when possessed of only an easy competence. If, however, this large property must be mine, I will spend only a small portion of it, and the remainder shall accumulate for those who may succeed me. But, perhaps, death will soon release this aching heart, and, if so, I shall die happy in the consciousness that I have not, willingly, been the means of depriving Lord Mayfield of that which I still believe to be his own."

Julia was now overcome by her emotions, and, assisted by Mrs. Markham, she left the room to seek rest and refreshment on her own couch. Her pitying friend would have remained by to soothe and console her, but this she would not permit, and when Mrs. Markham returned to the room in which they had left Lady Mayfield, she found her occupied in a train of melancholy thoughts.

"What course can we now adopt?" she exclaimed, on seeing her friend approach. "Julia seems resolute in her determination, and I fear no persuasion of ours will ever induce her to alter the views she has so unfortunately formed."

"There is but one hope," replied Mrs. Markham; "and to that I shall cling to the very last."

"What is it?"

'That she may marry the person to whom her heart is attached."

"Do you know the person?" asked Lady Mayfield, in a tone of anxiety.

"I have already acknowledged that Julia has made me her confidant," replied Mrs. Markham; "but when she did so, it was under a strict injunction that I should never betray the secret without her permission."

"'Tis most singular," exclaimed Lady Mayfield; "for on all other subjects she is so particularly ingenuous."

"Ay," answered Mrs. Markham; "but in these affairs of the heart young persons are more inclined to be secret and reserved even to their best friends."

"Judging from what you know," asked her ladyship, "do you think she will ever see this favoured lover again?"

"I do."

"Perhaps, though, at some very distant period?"

"I rather think it will not be many hours first," replied Mrs. Markham; and then, thinking she had said rather too much, she added, "I have no authority for saying so, and, perhaps, have spoken rather from my own hopes than any real foundation."

"My anxiety on this subject may appear strange to you," said Lady Mayfield ; "and yet, Heaven is my witness, that I have no design in it, except a fervent wish to see my niece as happy as she deserves to be. For some reason or other, she is a prey to melancholy ; an ill-requited love is the most probable cause, and in that case, the most likely way to remove it is by prevailing on her to accept the hand of some other suitor. Doubtless, she will have many when she begins to mix a little more in the gay world, and for that reason I have been particularly urgent in my request that she will accompany me in my next visit to London."

"I have been thinking," said Mrs. Markham, "that perhaps your son's arrival here may serve to make her a little more cheerful. They have met before, I believe, and who knows but they may now form an attachment for each other."

"I have already stated my objections to such a match," answered Lady Mayfield. "The world is ever ready to put false constructions on our actions ; and were such an event to take place, it would be at once said we brought about the union to serve our own ends. Lord Mayfield shall know my thoughts about this subject immediately after his arrival, and I know his honour too well to believe that any selfish views will induce him to seek Julia's hand for the sake of the fortune he has lost."

"But if they should really love each other," observed Mrs. Markham, "I see no reason why Lord Mayfield should not marry her."

"And even then," replied her ladyship, "it may be said that he threw himself in her way on purpose to try how far chance might favour him."

"Why need you care for the idle rumours of the world?" demanded Mrs. Markham. "The thought could only be engendered by those whose opinion is not worth caring for, whilst the match, I will undertake to say, would give satisfaction to all who really hold you in their regard."

"We seem to have forgotten," exclaimed Lady Mayfield, "that all this time we have been only building castles in the air. Julia may care no more for my son than any one else ; and, to speak the truth, I hope she may not, though I believe the consequence would be that he goes abroad, never, in all probability, to return during my lifetime. He will then have my dowry, in addition to his own fortune, and may once more mix in the gay society from which, till that period arrives, he will be driven."

The ringing of the first dinner-bell now interrupted the conversation, and the ladies repaired to their dressing-rooms to make the necessary alterations in their toilette. Lady Mayfield could not banish from her mind the uneasy reflections which recent events had given rise to, and on seating herself at the dinner-table she still exhibited signs of the anxiety with which she was oppressed. Mrs. Markham, however, took care to give the conversation a different turn, so that an hour or two afterwards the usual cheerfulness was restored.

CHAPTER XXII.

AN ARRIVAL.

THE next morning, before our heroine had left her room, she was surprised at receiving a visit from Mrs. Markham, whose countenance betrayed that she was the bearer of some important and pleasing intelligence. This was immediately perceived by Julia, who, unable to guess what it was, asked anxiously what had occurred to afford so much pleasure.

"Neither more nor less," answered the lady, "than the arrival of a visitor."

"A visitor !" cried Julia ; "is it a male or female ?"

"A male."

"Not such an one, then, I trust as Mr. Simon Briefly, the lawyer."

"No," replied Mrs. Markham ; "it is a person that I believe you will be glad to see ; and so, my love, to keep you no longer in suspense, our visitor is no other than Lord Mayfield."

"Lord Mayfield !" cried Julia, turning deadly pale ; "then I am, indeed, most unhappy. Yet, why should I say so when doubtless this visit is intended for his mother ?"

"Partly, I dare say," answered Mrs. Markham ; "though, between ourselves, I rather think he had somebody else in view when he turned his horse's head this way."

"Do you mean me ?" she asked.

"Indeed I do, my love," replied the lady ; "for almost his first inquiry was after you."

"Then it cannot be that he cares for me," exclaimed Julia ; "for the last interview we had together was decisive as to the opinion he has of me."

"Psha ! it was nothing but a lover's quarrel," replied Mrs. Markham ; "and they, as we all know, always terminate in making the parties better friends than ever. Of course he has seen his own folly, and is now anxious to see you and make it up."

"He has taken a long time to think of it, then," sighed our heroine ; "and, to speak my mind, my good friend, I have no desire to see him stoop so low as to ask my pardon for his offence, deeply as I felt the reproaches with which he loaded me. It was a sore trial, I will own, at first, but the pang has passed away, and, as I have told you, I am resolved never again to give my heart to any man."

"But he already possesses it," returned Mrs. Markham, "and I really do not see how you are to help yourself. Love, my dear girl, is not so easily conquered as you seem to imagine ; happen what may, there is always a portion of it lingering in the heart, and, take my word for it, you are no more exempt from a feeling of tenderness than the rest of your sex."

"I will not see him," exclaimed Julia.

"Nay, how can I deliver so cruel a message ?"

"Say that I am ill and cannot leave my chamber."

"Would you have me tell him a story ?"

"It would be no story," replied Julia ; "for the news of his arrival has indeed made me feel ill."

"Then it is with joy," exclaimed Mrs. Markham ; "for, try to disguise it from yourself as you will, I am bold to say that nothing could have afforded you greater satisfaction than the news I have brought. You feel a little agitated, perhaps, but that will wear off, and then I know you will so far oblige me as to go down and see his lordship."

"Indeed, indeed, I cannot," cried Julia.

"Oh, but you will presently."

"Nay, you must make some excuse for me."

"What excuse can I make, if he is determined to see you ?" asked Mrs. Markham. "He will very likely stay here three or four days, and we cannot keep you upon the sick list all that time, you know."

"He cannot wish to see me," cried Julia. "The anger we parted in affords me sufficient reason to believe that he no longer loves me."

"Ay," returned her friend, "but the affair about the miniature has been thoroughly explained by his mother, and of course, as a man of honour, he feels himself bound to make a proper apology. Depend on it, my experience in the world is sufficient to set me right upon the point, and if you only grant him half an hour's interview, he will not only offer a satisfactory explanation of his conduct, but reinstate himself in your heart just as he was before this little rumpus between you took place."

"Indeed, my dear madam, you must find some excuse for me," cried Julia. "I have made up my mind never to see him again, and that was one reason why I objected to visit London with Lady Mayfield."

"I am not generally obdurate," replied Mrs. Markham, "but in this instance I cannot be a bearer of excuses. His lordship certainly expects to see you, and surely my dear Julia will not suffer him to depart from my house under the impression that he has offended her beyond forgiveness."

" Say to him that he has long since been forgiven," cried Julia; " but do not urge me to permit an interview that must be painful to us both."

" But the pain will wear away, and then you will be happy in the restoration of each other's love," replied Mrs. Markham. " I know you think me too urgent in this matter, but I see that your happiness depends upon the meeting, and I am not willing to throw away so excellent an opportunity."

" Does Lady Mayfield know that you have come on this errand?"

" Oh, yes, certainly," answered her friend; " and, if I may judge by her looks, she was well pleased at hearing her son make such anxious inquiries after you."

" Ah! then she knows of our former acquaintance."

" Not from me, at any rate," exclaimed Mrs. Markham; " for, though I have often longed to tell her all I knew upon the subject, the promise I gave checked me, and I have been obliged to witness the unhappiness of all parties, without being permitted to put forth a helping hand to any party."

" Yet now," cried Julia, " all, I fear, will be discovered."

" And high time it should be so," replied her friend, " since this foolish coolness has lasted quite long enough in all conscience."

" It will last still longer," replied our heroine; " for I must again entreat you to make the best excuse to his lordship for not seeing him."

" He will take no refusal, if he loves you as much as I imagine."

" Nay, have I not proof that he has long since ceased to love me?"

" I don't know what you would bring forward as proof," answered Mrs. Markham; " but, in my opinion, the very circumstance of his coming here is positive evidence that he does love you as much as ever."

" Would that I could prevail on you to spare me the pain of this interview."

" My dear girl, there is nothing to dread," returned her friend. " Matters will go smoothly enough if you will only allow them, and as for his lordship, if he has been guilty of a little rudeness, and is now sorry for it, he ought to be forgiven."

" I do forgive him," replied Julia; " but that assurance may be as well conveyed to him by you as by myself."

" He would not thank me for being a go-between," answered Mrs. Markham. " His object is to see you, that he may ask pardon for himself, and if you only tell him that the past is forgotten, he will soon find eloquence enough to make you receive him into the same favour as formerly. Nay, have you not confessed to me that you can never give your heart to anybody else; and is it to be imagined after that acknowledgment, that I can take a message which would most likely be the means of making you unhappy for life."

" Nay, have I not said that my chief solace will be to pass the remainder of my days in your society?"

" Ay, but that was at a time when you had no reason to believe that Lord Mayfield would take so much pains to procure your pardon. People are apt to say foolish things sometimes, but it does not follow that they are to abide by them, when they see that they have acted with indiscretion."

" You will at least acknowledge that the quarrel was not of my seeking?"

" I see no great quarrel in it," replied Mrs. Markham. " He found a miniature which bore a great resemblance to you, but, as since appears, was taken for your mother. He grew jealous about it, and as you could afford no satisfactory explanation, there seemed to be something like a confirmation of his doubts. He spoke rather too harshly, perhaps, but what of that, if he afterwards come to own his fault, and ask your forgiveness?"

" And that," said our heroine, " he could have received either through his mother or yourself."

" Ay," returned her friend; " but there is nothing like receiving the confirmation from the fountain head. Besides, he may have some other things to say, which would come awkwardly through any other channel. So now come with me, for I see his lordship is walking in the garden, and with your permission, I will lead you to him."

Julia found that it would be vain to offer any further resistance to the well-meant kindness of her friend, and taking her arm, they proceeded to the place where Lord Mayfield was anxiously pacing up and down. He advanced on seeing them, and then Mrs. Markham slipping away, left them to their *tete-a-tete*. Julia would have sunk to the earth but for the timely aid of his lordship, and then stammering out an apology for the trouble she had occasioned, she would have retreated, but for the gentle restraint he used."

" Nay, leave me not, dearest Julia," he exclaimed; " at least not till I have obtained your forgiveness for an affront that I have not yet pardoned myself."

" There is no need for apology, my lord," she faintly replied. " My friend told me you wished for a parting interview ere you leave England. If you are indeed about to quit your native land, I am sorry for it, since I, perhaps, am the cause. For your mother's sake I hope you will change your resolution."

" To part from her," he replied, " is indeed a source of the deepest affliction; but having seen every hope vanish, I must now endure it with gratitude. But I am occupying your time, Lady Stanmore, and will therefore only ask your forgiveness for the violence I was guilty of when last we met. I sinned most grievously, but my punishment has borne some proportion to the magnitude of my offence."

" That, my lord," she replied, " has long since been forgotten."

" Your generosity overwhelms me," exclaimed Lord Mayfield, with emotion. " I have been most unhappy, yet even in exile I shall bear with me the remembrance of her whom I had once hoped to make my wife."

" What!" she cried, " would you have accepted the hand of the once lowly Julia Dawson?"

" Ay," he replied; " possessed of your love, my happiness would be complete."

" My assent then, would make you happy?"

" It would."

" Then it is yours," she exclaimed, in scarcely articulate accents; " you may blame my precipitation, my lord, but I have spoken thus freely, only because I know that your departure would entail endless misery."

At this moment the Countess of Mayfield and Mrs. Markham returned. The former was still weeping, but no sooner did she observe the altered aspect of her son's countenance, than guessing that some favourable explanation had taken place, she eagerly inquired if he had resolved upon postponing his journey for the present.

" I have," he replied, joyfully; " and if the change in my determination affords happiness to my mother, let her thanks be given to Lady Julia, who has consented to restore peace to a heart that but a few minutes since was overloaded with sorrow."

" Then for ever blessed be the interview," cried Mrs. Markham, " for my hopes are now fulfilled."

" What mean your words, my dear son?" exclaimed the countess, as she recovered from her surprise.

" My dear Julia," he replied, " has at length consented to give me her hand."

" And thus secures her own happiness," exclaimed Mrs. Markham. " Ah, my dear Julia, you may look cross at me if you please, but the interdiction you laid upon me has been removed, and I am now at liberty to declare how long you have secretly loved his lordship."

" My dear friend," cried the blushing girl, earnestly; " do not, I implore you, speak of the past. You have been my confidant—in your bosom every secret of my heart has been reposed, and it would cover me with confusion were his lordship to hear all the romantic follies I have been guilty of."

Happiness seemed to be now completely restored, and the postboys, who had been slowly driving round the lawn all this time, were ordered to dismount, and put up their horses till they received further instructions from their master. As for Lord Mayfield, the transition from sadness to joy was so sudden, that he could scarcely convince himself the whole was not a dream. Julia, too, seemed to live anew. The peace which for many years had been a stranger to her, now appeared to have permanently taken up its abode in her bosom, and her countenance became calm and happy. Never had she seemed more beautiful than at this moment, which was the happiest of her life.

CHAPTER XXIII.

THE next morning Julia was seated alone, and having no longer a sorrow to afflict her heart, she gave way to the natural impulse of her spirits, and sang one of those songs which she had so much delighted in, ere she had been crushed beneath the weight of her afflictions. So intently, indeed, was she thus engaged, that she was not conscious of any one's presence, till Lord Mayfield suddenly presented himself before her. He instantly perceived the surprise into which he had thrown her, and taking her hand, said,—

" You will pardon me, I trust, my dearest Julia, for thus abruptly breaking in upon your solitude."

" I was amusing myself by trying to remember the words of a once favourite song," she replied, with a sigh. " Months have passed away since I could find spirit enough to occupy myself in the same way."

" Ay, dearest," he replied ; " but from this time forward, grief shall no longer oppress your heart. I, perhaps, have had some share in strewing your path with thorns, but the recollections of what you have endured shall prompt me in future to blot from your memory every thought that may serve to bring back the remembrance of the past."

The two elder ladies now made their appearance, and as soon as the morning's meal was concluded, Lady Mayfield proposed, as the weather was exceedingly beautiful, that they should go to Stanmore Castle.

" It will serve to occupy our time most agreeably," she added ; " and it is, in fact, necessary, my dear Julia, that you should visit the place as its future mistress."

" And i am certain," interposed Mrs. Markham, " that you, my lady, will not resign possession of it to our young friend grudgingly. His lordship, too, I suppose, will shortly find a home in the ancient mansion of his ancestors."

" I have discovered," exclaimed Lord Mayfield, " that a few hours can make a singular alteration in one's determination. Yesterday I would have resigned all without a sigh, but now, since it is to be shared with my dear Julia, I feel most happy in the prospect of becoming the master of a domain that for centuries has been the favourite abode of my forefathers."

" Indeed, my lord," cried Julia, " I am not quite certain that you are indebted to me for it. At present I have not assumed the right to dispose of it, nor shall I ever regard it as my own inheritance, till I am convinced that Lady Mayfield is not making too great a sacrifice by yielding it up."

Everything was soon in readiness for setting out on the little excursion, but for some reason or other, Mrs. Markham declined making one of the party. The excuse she made was, that Sir Edward Digby had intimated his intention of paying her a visit, but the most probable cause was, that she wished not to interpose her presence at such a juncture.

" Another time," she said, " will be more convenient to all parties; in short, you must first settle it between you, who is to be its legal possessor, and when I am assured that Lord Mayfield is to be master there, I shall no longer defer a visit that must confer so much happiness on me. So remember, Julia, everything depends upon you, and I therefore leave the rest to your own judgment."

" Dear Mrs. Markham," cried his lordship, in a voice agitated with gratitude, " what a fortunate thing it is for a man who is too modest to give utterance to his own ardent wishes, to have so generous a friend whose influence over Julia is so powerful."

" Ah !" exclaimed our heroine, shaking her head playfully, " and thus it is then, that I am to be abandoned by a friend in whom I placed the greatest reliance. I thought you would at least be neuter, but just when your aid is most required, I find that you are taking part against me."

" The truth is," replied Mrs. Markham, " I am taking this course because I believe it to be most conducive to your happiness."

" And will it at the same time add to your own ?" asked his lordship.

" I love her as my own daughter," replied Mrs. ▉arkham, "and from the first moment of our meeting, my affection was bestowed upon her. Our acquaintance has now lasted some few months, and it is, therefore, from experience I can declare that the more your lordship knows of her inestimable qualities, the more will you have reason to bless the hour which made you acquainted. I have now ceased to wonder at the sympathetic affection I instantly formed for her. My heart comprehended, though my reason was unconscious of it, that she was the child of him who had been the object of my earliest affection. Yet, when I have

See p. 64.

since ascertained that the child and her mother were exact counterparts of each other, could I longer blame him for a choice that was so likely to ensure his own ▉piness. Observe the difference between us, and then say if it can be wondered ▉t her father made choice of one whose beauty so far surpassed my own."

▉ Alas !" sighed Julia, " had my unhappy parent known, as I do, the heart of my dear Mrs. Markham, he would not have forsaken her for either beauty or riches.   But he was young and inexperienced, and therein lies his chief excuse."

By this time the carriage was driven up to the door, in which Lady Mayfiled, Julia, the two Miss Markhams, and Lord Mayfield, seated themselves to proceed on the excursion that had been proposed.

The carriage rolled rapidly along the well-kept road that swept through the park, and then entered a long avenue, bordered on each side by tall elms, whose grateful shadows sheltered the little party from the heat of the noon-day sun.

On every side of them opened the most beautiful of all prospects—the rich corn-fields, and the green fresh meadows of that fertile county.   A refreshing shower had fallen in the morning, and everything around—tree, bush, and shrub, wore a freshness of appearance cheering to the eye.   A sudden turning in the road disclosed to them, at the distance of some three or four miles, and perched on a slight eminence, the mansion to which they were proceeding.   The upper part of the house rose above a thick mass of foliage in which it was embosomed, and formed one of the most striking objects in the landscape, to which it added considerably in effect.

As Mrs. Markham's eye caught sight of its well-known embattled roof, a shade of sadness came over her countenance, and she sank back in the carriage, apparently giving way to recollections of days fraught to her with both joy and sorrow.

The rest of the party observed this, and as it was known that one of the most painful events in the early life of Mrs. Markham was connected with that building, no one ventured to interrupt her, and one by one they relapsed into silence, amusing themselves with observing and admiring the beauties that nature with a lavish hand, had spread around them.

It was evident that Mrs. Markham's meditations, though they had called up scenes and characters to which she had long endeavoured to school her mind to forgetfulness, had a favourable effect upon her frame, for a placidity stole over her features, giving them the most gentle and benevolent expression ; and though

> " Through the shadowy past,
> Like a tomb-searcher, Memory ran,
> Lifting each shroud that Time had cast
> O'er buried hopes,"

yet to her mind it brought no pang of self-reproach—no remorse for one act in her sinless and useful life.

At last Mrs. Markham appeared, by an effort, to shake off the reverie into which she had fallen, and turning to the Countess of Mayfield, she said,—

" My dear madam, the subject of which I am about to speak, I am aware, must be of painful interest to us both, and, perhaps, for the moment, may cause us pangs which we expected never again to feel.   For years I have wished to ask what I now request you to relate to me.   I would know from your lips the particulars of your life that refer immediately to the period preceding the marriage of the unfortunate Lord Kendal, your brother, and his beautiful bride, the equally unfortunate Ellen Darnley."

" My dear Mrs. Markham," returned the Countess of Mayfield, in a gentle tone, " I would have told you ere this, but for fear I should be giving you unnecessary pain."

Mrs. Markham pressed her hand, and with a look of gratitude thanked her for her kind consideration.

" I knew your sensitive heart," continued the countess, " and I felt sure that, though years had passed, and you had become the wife of another, you still cherished feelings for him who had so recklessly destroyed the hopes of your youthful mind, which were little, if at all, blunted by time."

" Nay," cried Mrs. Markham, " I can well understand the delicacy and kindness that prompt this hesitation ; but be assured I have nerved myself to whatever you may have to relate.   I am convinced that it was vain to

continuance of your brother's love after he became acquainted with Ellen Darnley, and can therefore listen with composure to the recital of all that occurred."

"Well, then, since it is your wish, I will no longer hesitate," answered her ladyship. "Of course you remember that a sisterly attachment subsisted between myself and poor Ellen Darnley. We were never happy but in each other's society. The close neighbourhood of her father's mansion to Marchmont House, where I lived with my grandmother, occasioned our acquaintance in early childhood, and as years rolled over, the feeling grew into the warmest attachment. My brother had also known her from a child, but I believe never regarded her otherwise than as a playmate, till he met her some years afterwards about the period when I was to be married. Being reared in the Roman Catholic faith, her father wished her to take the veil, but the design was always strongly opposed by her, and the consequence was that the differences arose between them which rendered home anything but comfortable to her.

"Under these circumstances, it is not much to be wondered at that she preferred my company to that of her father, by whom she was subjected to a degree of harshness that almost amounted to cruelty ; indeed, he seemed well pleased at being rid of one for whom he had ceased to feel affection, and she remained with us sometimes for weeks together, without any inquiry being made about her.

"She had been informed of my brother's engagement, and, little dreaming of the mischief that was to follow, appeared to regard him only as the brother of the friend whom she esteemed beyond all the world beside. The situation in which poor Ellen was placed was, it is true, one of extreme danger to a heart so warm and susceptible as hers. In the course of time she began to find that his image was not to be easily banished from her mind, and, in spite of every effort, she found that it was impossible to check the growing partiality that my brother's suavity of manners had excited in his behalf. Nor was his own situation less dangerous than hers, for he was charmed with her beauty, and on each occasion of his visits to our house, he found it more and more difficult to tear himself from her presence.

"About that period, the increasing neglect of my husband became insupportable, and, unfortunately for the peace of all parties, I prevailed on my brother to stay with us as often as possible, in order to dispel the melancholy thoughts with which I was afflicted. I spent most of my time between them and my infant son, whilst my lord sought amusement and dissipation in scenes which served to drive from his mind all thoughts save those which tended to his inordinate love of pleasure.

"At home we were happy in each other's society ; but at length it seemed as if Lord Kendal began to discover the danger into which he was running, for, on a sudden, he left us, with an excuse that business, of an urgent nature, required his immediate presence at home. Indeed, as we afterwards found out, he resolved to fulfil the duty which honour demanded of him ; but, as it soon proved, his heart was irrecoverably lost. Ellen drooped during his absence, and as a serious illness followed, I wrote to him requesting his immediate return. He came ; my young friend speedily revived, and, to be brief with this part of my narrative, they were, within a few weeks, privately married.

"Shortly afterwards, the bridegroom visited his father ; but when he returned to us, after being discarded as an outcast, never shall I forget the scene of grief and despair that took place between us. As it was impossible for him to remain in England, I prevailed upon him to accept a small portion of my own income to support them on the continent, till affairs should take a more favourable turn. They went, I believe, to reside with a relative of Ellen, who was then a widow. Alas ! how afflicting to me was their absence, for in what way could I excuse my own conduct in having been the means of bringing about this unfortunate marriage ?

"To add to my mental sufferings, I soon discovered that, though united to the woman whom he almost idolised, Lord Kendal was far from being happy. He could not conceal from himself the fact that he had been guilty of deceiving the woman he had promised to make his wife, and the thoughts of her unhappiness were a continual reproach that haunted every moment of his life. This, added to the curses of an incensed father, filled his soul with sadness, so that even the attentions of his faithful wife could scarcely ever induce him to resume, even for a moment, the joyfulness of spirits for which he was once so conspicuous.

"At length, when he found that Ellen was in a situation to make him a parent at no very distant period, his melancholy became more intense than ever. He would not, however, confess even to his wife, the cause of this despair ; but I believe there is no doubt that he believed the curses which had been heaped upon his own head would descend upon the innocent offspring of an union that had been contracted in too much haste."

"Alas !" interrupted Julia, "the curses of his offended parent did, indeed, long rest upon me."

"The great dislike which my father bore to the Roman Catholic church," resumed Lady Mayfield, "prompted him to extend his curse to his posterity, believing that it would prove the only effectual mode of inducing the parents to bring up their children in the Protestant faith. He had been informed that the Darnleys were excessively zealous in the cause of their own religion, and, dreading the influence of Ellen over her fond and confiding husband, he was induced so to make his will that none of his property should descend to any of his grandchildren, unless they were brought up in the reformed faith.

"Lord Kendal had ever entertained a truly filial regard for his parent, and nothing could exceed his grief when he discovered that not a hope remained of his restoration to favour. He then began to reflect upon the mischief which he had thus brought upon himself and his wife, and though he still loved his unfortunate partner with unabated affection, he could not suppress the bitter regrets that his present situation gave rise to. Ellen was less affected by their altered circumstances than himself, because she felt assured that the enmity of Lord Stanmore would gradually give way to the love with which he had ever regarded his son. But these anticipations were doomed never to be realised, for there were some points upon which my father was immoveable, and on none was he more so than when the religion he professed was concerned.

"At length, when news reached me that Ellen was in a situation to give a child to her husband, I purchased everything that would be required in her confinement, and these I sent off, together with a quantity of apparel, for the expected babe. The latter articles I made with my own hands, well knowing that that circumstance would render the present a more acceptable one. To this circumstance it is tha I am enabled to identify the infant's apparel in which Julia was discovered by her generous benefactor, Mr. Dawson. Thus, you perceive, on how trivial a thing some of the most important events of our lives may be made to turn.

"In the course of a few weeks afterwards, I received a letter from my brother, informing me that his wife had presented him with a daughter, and that both the mother and infant were going on favourably. He then went on to speak of Lord Stanmore, whose death had taken place only a few days before, and who had yielded up his latest breath without expressing the slightest regret for the rupture that had occurred between him and his repentant son.

"The letter of my brother manifested a very sincere feeling of grief that his father had thus retained his anger to the last moment of existence. The regret, I believe, was not so much occasioned by the poverty he was devoted to endure, as by the consciousness that the curses of an offended parent had been called down by his own wilful obstinacy. The title became his as a matter of course, but he would have been better without it, since poverty would disable him from supporting the dignity, and he would thus become an object of the mingled scorn and pity of all those who knew that his fallen condition had been produced by his own want of discretion.

"Shortly after this I again heard from him, and from that letter I learned that he intended to return to England as soon as he could make the necessary arrangements for the removal of his family. Several dark hints were thrown out that his situation abroad was far from comfortable, and from expressions which were here and there dropped, it was evident that he alluded to plots which had been formed against him. What these exactly were, I could not clearly understand, but it seemed that Ellen's confessor had made more than one attempt to carry off the infant, in order that she might be instructed in the Roman Catholic doctrines. This is likely enough, for in countries where one of the parents differs from the national religion, there is always great anxiety lest the offspring should be brought up as a heretic.

" Nor did he believe his own situation a very safe one, for he had been repeatedly urged by the priests to conform to their religion; as he still continued faithful to that in which he had been brought up, they even proceeded to threaten him with their vengeance, and spies were set to watch, in order that any expression he might make use of should form a pretext for commencing a criminal prosecution against him for disrespect for their church. Once, indeed, he had suffered a short imprisonment, and it was only upon the remonstrance of the English ambassador that he was set at liberty. Under these circumstances, he thought it most prudent to return with as little delay as possible, and he told me that arrangements were in progress to forward this design.

" Three weeks afterwards I received another communication from him, by which I learned that everything was now in readiness for his departure from the continent, and that, assisted by the money I had sent over in the meanwhile, he hoped to reach England by the next vessel that sailed. It seemed, too, that his situation rendered it necessary for him to maintain the strictest secrecy even to Ellen, for her friends had obtained so powerful a mastery over her mind, that there was every reason to believe she would refuse to accompany him, unless it were under the impression that their visit to this country was intended to be a merely temporary one. To guard as much as possible against suspicion, he prevailed upon Ellen to remove with him to Calais, but this she refused to do, unless accompanied by her confessor, and the female relative with whom they had been living.

" Being thus driven to deception, he formed a project by which he might lull their suspicions, and amongst other things he pretended to be in treaty for a small house, preferring, as he said, a residence by the seaside, to one in the interior of the country. Having thus succeeded in avoiding the doubts which would have marred his design, he secretly took a passage in an English ship for his family and one female domestic, whose attachment for the child rendered her a valuable acquisition in their present almost friendless condition. Ellen was not to know anything about these arrangements till the very last moment, and as it was feared she would refuse to leave the country, it was resolved that my brother should propose a boat excursion, when all might be put on board the vessel just as she was about to set sail.

" Anxiously did I look for the next communication, and when at length it arrived, I was informed that the day following the one on which the letter was dated, my brother was to put his long cherished project into execution. Joyfully did he anticipate the moment that was to reunite us, and with no less pleasure did I look forward to a meeting that would afford us much mutual affection. But, alas! how short-sighted are mortals! the vessel was never to reach its place of destination, and after a week of anxious suspense, news was brought that a vessel had been wrecked off the Sussex coast, and neither crew nor passengers had been saved. That the ill-fated ship was the one in which my brother and his family had sailed there could be no doubt, and giving myself up to sorrow, I mourned in secret the hapless fate which had snatched from me all that I had ever held dearest in the world.

" Little did I think that one was saved from the tempest of that fearful night. All, I thought, had been swept away by the devastating power of the elements, yet the Ocean Child was spared, and after many long and anxious years have passed away, it has pleased Heaven to restore to me the child of my beloved brother. The clothes in which you were found, my dear Julia, confirm the truth of my assertion. They were worked by my own hands, and, if called upon to do so, I can swear they are those I made for you."

" This discovery is, indeed, a most gratifying one," cried Julia, throwing her arms round the neck of Lady Mayfield. " I believed myself without one relation in the world, yet, when least expected, do I find in you a second mother."

"And a mother I will ever be to you, my dear girl," cried her ladyship. "Even from the first, your resemblance to my unfortunate Ellen filled me with confusion ; I felt as if a new dawn of hope had opened before me, and the event has fully realised the expectation in which I so freely indulged."

The two Miss Markhams and Lord Mayfield had listened with the greatest interest to the recital given by the countess, and all were gratified to find that, instead of depressing, it had tended greatly to calm the spirits of Mrs. Markham, upon whose countenance now sat an expression of serenity, to which it had long been a stranger.

The remainder of the ride was delightful, and when at length they reached the castle and dismounted, the youngest of Mrs. Markham's daughters, taking the arm of Lord Mayfield, said, with a mixture of playfulness and sorrow,—

"Come this way with me, my lord, and I will show you the portrait of a gentleman, who, they tell me, was to have been my papa."

Lord Mayfield almost mechanically accompanied the young lady, who had no sooner reached the apartment in which the pictures were, than raising her hands with astonishment, she exclaimed,—

"Why, I declare it is a likeness of yourself; it is your own portrait! Ah! I can no longer wonder, then, that Julia was so struck with it when we came here once before. Don't you remember," she added, turning to our heroine, " how pale you turned on seeing this picture?"

Lord Mayfield listened with intense rapture to these few words ; but his attention was soon called off by seeing the tears which rose to Julia's eyes, whilst her bosom heaved with the contending emotions which filled it. He immediately hastened from the room for a glass of water, and returning instantly, supplicated her most earnestly to drink it.

"It is very foolish of me to yield to these emotions," she at length cried, on partially recovering herself. "I was taken by surprise, but the weakness has yielded, and, indeed, my lord, I already feel better."

"Dearest Julia !" he exclaimed, "I am not sorry to see this emotion, since the indulgence of it will prove a release to you."

By this time the old housekeeper came into the room, and observing in the person of our heroine the fair young creature whom she so well recollected, she started back with amazement and delight.

"You are, doubtless, surprised at this unexpected visit, my good woman," exclaimed Lord Mayfield ; "but you may remember that when I was here last, I told you it was probable that I should soon order the old castle to be put into habitable repair. Even at that period my ardent wishes prompted me to hope that the time would soon arrive when I should present this young lady as your future mistress."

"Is she not Lady Stanmore, my lord?" asked the old woman, with some hesitation.

"Most certainly she is," he replied. "But, instead of making her the mistress of this domain, she has promised, ere long, to make me its master."

"And a happy day it will be when it arrives," cried the housekeeper ; "for then shall I indeed live over the time that I have so often regretted."

Julia still sat with her eyes intently fixed upon the portrait of her unfortunate father, and Lord Mayfield, anxious to give another direction to her thoughts, prevailed upon her to accompany him through the pleasure-grounds, which were still kept in all their former neatness. Lady Mayfield, for reasons of her own, that it may be presumed were considerate for the lovers, preferred staying where she was, and the two young ladies, from similar motives, stopped behind to keep her company.

How delightfully to Lord Mayfield did the time pass away whilst Julia and he strolled through the grounds, intent only upon the conversation that ensued between them. So unconscious were they, indeed, of the fleeting moments, that their absence from the house was longer than had been intended, and it was not till Lady Mayfield sent to remind them that it was time they should depart that they were conscious of having passed more than a few minutes in each other's company.

The sole purpose that Mrs. Markham had in remaining at home that morning was, in fact, to prepare her nephew to receive Lord Mayfield as the accepted lover of Lady Stanmore. Not to have endured a severe pang on receiving this intelligence, would have proved Sir Edward highly unworthy the regard in which he was held. He, however, sustained the shock with tolerable firmness, and, aided by his own sense of honour, he prepared himself to meet his noble rival, rather as a friend who had made Julia happy, than as one who had deprived him of a chance which he had clung to in despite of the positive rejection he had met with from her.

To be next in her esteem he regarded as an inestimable honour; and, on the other hand, she had made such favourable mention of Sir Edward's disinterested regard for her, in the vindication of her character even after she had refused to accept his addresses, that Lord Mayfield was anxious to make acquaintance with a man whose character was in every way so deserving of respect.

Being thus favourably disposed towards each other, not the slightest trace of rivalry or ill-feeling could be discovered when they met. The kind attention which Lord Mayfield showed towards our heroine, evinced only a decided preference without that ostentatious display so frequently manifested by lovers, and which would have proved so painful to the rejected suitor.

Thus passed away the whole week that Sir Edward Digby remained with them, and long before the termination of that period, so charmed was he by the conciliating manner of Lord Mayfield, that he freely confessed to himself that, since Julia could not be his, there was no other man to whom he would so willingly have surrendered her.

"Some weak, disappointed lovers," he exclaimed, in the most perfect good humour, "would no doubt have hung or shot themselves; I, however, have yielded to my destiny, and by doing so, have laid the foundation of a friendship that promises to yield me an abundance of gratification. Indeed," he added, "so completely have I conquered my affection, that, if Lady Stanmore will allow me the honour, I shall feel the greatest pleasure in presenting her hand to you at the altar."

Julia, who was present during this conversation, looked her grateful acknowledgment, and after a few moments, said,—

"Nothing, believe me, can afford me greater satisfaction than to accept the offer, if my kind and dear friend, Mr. Barton, will also agree to it. He has been as a father to me, and would have adopted the friendless Ocean Child when there were few willing to undertake a charge of such responsibility."

"Ay, ay, e'en as you will," exclaimed the old gentleman, who formed one of the happy group. "I certainly did anticipate the pleasure of acting the part of a father on the happy day, but I shall be quite satisfied with being present, and nothing will afford me more gratification than to see his lordship receive the hand of his bride from a generous, high-minded rival."

Shortly after this an agreeable addition was made to the party by the arrival of Mr. Capel, his wife, and daughter. Unfortunately, however, Mrs. Markham had not room to accommodate all her visitors, and in this difficulty Sir Edward Digby invited the two young ladies to become partakers of his hospitality. The offer was gladly accepted, and thus commenced the foundation of an acquaintance that the worthy baronet had good reason afterwards to congratulate himself upon.

Lord Mayfield, meantime, had not been idle in forwarding the preliminary articles necessary for the approaching nuptials; and it was stipulated that the sum of three thousand a year, which Julia had limited to herself, should be allotted for her own private fortune.

Matters having been thus far arranged, his lordship became more urgent than ever that she would name an early period for the union which he had so much at heart. Julia at first hesitated to do this, but, upon reflection, she saw so much reason to anticipate happiness in the marriage state, that she abstained from making excuses which would only have arisen from an affectation that she deemed unwor-

the character it had ever been her pride to maintain. She could easily see, too, that every word, look, and action, proved the entire devotedness of his love, though it was displayed in a manner so mild and gentle that each hour her regard for him increased both in power and intensity.

Emma Capel, to whom we must now refer, was, both in form and features, exceedingly beautiful. Sir Edward Digby, when a youth, had received his education from her father, and even at that early period of their lives, a partiality had grown up between them which even during absence had not been entirely forgotten. Her manner was simple and unaffected, and the personal charms with which she was gifted were greatly improved by the excellent instruction she had received from her father. It is not, therefore, to be wondered at if Sir Edward now felt a renewal of his former attachment ; for, since she had come on a visit to Mrs. Markham, they were thrown frequently into each other's society, and, indeed, were scarcely happy unless together.

This was not unobserved by Julia, who thus saw, with the highest satisfaction, that the excellent baronet was likely to forget his previous disappointment in the more successful choice that he had now made. She had learned to regard Sir Edward as a favourite brother, and if she entertained one wish more than another, it was to see him happily settled in life.

At the time which had been appointed, Sir Edward Digby performed the office of father to our heroine, and then secured the promise of the happy bridegroom to do him the same kindly office at the expiration of a few weeks. Of course he had previously obtained the consent of both Emma Capel and her father ; the former of whom, without any affected prudery, had frankly acknowledged that he alone was the master of her affection.

It is unnecessary to trace the history of our heroine any further, since we have at length seen her in the possession of all that happiness which, at one period of her life, seemed to be hopeless. The narrative contains many incidents that are to be met with in every day life ; and our purpose will have been fully accomplished if the perusal of the foregoing pages should serve to convince the reader that difficulties should not deter us from pursuing the right course, and that the trials we may have to endure are generally succeeded by the happiness to which we all of us aspire.

THE END.

London : Printed and Published by E. Lloyd, 12, Salisbury-square, Fleet-street.

www.ingramcontent.com/pod-product-compliance
Lightning Source LLC
Chambersburg PA
CBHW081212170626
46811CB00010B/3251